Love,

Light,

and

Violet

Also by Lynn Renz

"Happy Magical Dreams" a Children's book under the pen name Lynn Brown.

They danced to the sound of raindrops
hitting the creek, like a secret drum.
As water hit the stones,
each droplet made a different sound,
a different note.
They danced in the rain
for what seemed like hours.
Merin twirled Violet in circles
as they danced their own secret dance.

LYNN RENZ

"LOVE LIGHT and VIOLET"
Copyright © 2018 NewSoft Publishing
First Edition
Editor and Interior Layout: Sybil Watts
Cover: Lynn Renz
Author Photo: Madison Brown
Interior Images: Various Artists

Published by
NewSoft Publishing
1355 Bardstown Road • Louisville, Kentucky 40204

Printed in the United States of America

Library of Congress Control Number: 2018909984

ISBN 13: 978-0-692-17628-3
ISBN 10: 0692176284

Love, Light and Violet

Violet Learns the Truth of Real Magic

by Lynn Renz

NewSoft Publishing

Louisville, Kentucky, US of A

Table of Contents

Dedication

I am grateful to all my lessons and blessings, without both I would not be who I am today.

This book is dedicated to everyone that has been there for me on this journey called Human Life.

- My parents for supporting me and being my biggest cheerleaders.
- My son for being my star in the night and inspiration for magic.
- My husband, Joe, for supporting me, and loving me as I am and for giving me my step-daughter Emily, whom I love as my own.
- All my family and friends – I love all of you. Thank you!
- Ms. Donna Ladd, for inspiring me to write at such a young age.
- To Mariel, for standing in the cold for me to photograph you for the cover. I hope you know how awesome you look on the cover. ☺
- My editor and publisher, Sybil. Thank you for being so awesome! You helped make my book come alive and for that I'm forever grateful that we met.

Last, but not least, I give all thanks and gratitude to my Creator and to Mother Earth for the inspirations in everyday life and nature.

Thank you, the reader, for going on this journey with me! I hope you enjoy reading the story of Violet as much as I have enjoyed writing it for you.

A note to the reader:

You have magic within you, it is inside of your heart.

Love, light and kindness *is* magic.

Magic is something that not everyone understands, or even believes in.

It is up to each of us to show the world that love and kindness do exist.

Magic is alive!

. . . . Magic never died.

~ Leonard Cohen

Chapter 1

The Fairyland Portal

As the night was beginning to fall, the moon began to awaken. The moon was a gorgeous light. She would sing a song that called to a young girl named Violet. Violet was a beautiful girl, even though she never believed or could see it herself. She was around 5'3', with shoulder-length, dark black hair It was the night before the last day of her junior year of high school, when the moon called to her once again, just like she always did. Violet sometimes felt like she was crazy, because she could hear the sweetest melodies in her head at night – it had even cured her insomnia.

Violet felt as though she was alone and yet not alone, at the same time. Her parents always worked or were always away on vacation, so she rarely ever saw them.

As she lay down to sleep at night, Violet would close her eyes, waiting for the melody to put her to sleep, which it did, as if on a schedule. Violet was never alone with these energies surrounding her. She felt no one would ever understand, and she wouldn't tell a soul because they would think she was crazy. They would have her put in an institution!

Violet used to have insomnia, due to night terrors – men chasing her or evil darkness lurking in closets and dark corners. She would stay awake listening to music, watching TV or reading a book, hoping she would fall asleep. Violet could hear people mumbling and footsteps throughout the house even though she was the only one there. Eventually she started to pay attention and listen; she could actually hear the spirit of the moon singing to her. It always sang a song of happiness and serenity that eased her to sleep. As she began to hear and listen to the song of the Moon, the night terrors ceased and she no longer suffered with insomnia.

Violet was a quiet teenager, unlike most loud-mouth, hormone-raging girls her age. Most people who crossed her path adored her, yet she only had a few close friends that knew her well;

well fairly well anyway. They were the type of friends that were able to drag out the fun, playful side of her. They could bring out a person not many knew existed, and that is exactly how she preferred things to be – a mystery.

Violet was a shy one and hated being in crowds and situations in which it would be hard for her to escape. She just wanted to stay in the house or garden and write her poetry and read her books. Books, for her, were a portal to a world far away from where she was – anywhere was better than here.

The night before her last day of school before summer break, she felt the Moon's presence and her energy called Violet to walk outside. As Violet got up from her reading corner, it was as if she were in a daze. Her hands reached to slide open the door to her back porch. Violet felt a cool breeze blowing in the night. She grabbed her purple coat off the hook that hung on the wall next to the door. The coat was very special to her as grandpa had given it to her for her 16th birthday, not too long ago. It kept her warm, just like his hugs did when he wrapped his arms around her.

The back of the house faced a wild garden that had not been ruined by man. This garden was full of what some would call weeds, however, Violet saw them as flowers and they were beautiful to her. When her family first moved in, she asked her dad not to cut the pathway, rather to just allow it to grow wild. He promised that he wouldn't cut it. The Garden became her getaway. On this 25th day of May, the moon sang the most beautiful song that she had ever heard.

> *"Come to me my child and rest awhile,*
> *there is no need to fear for I am here.*
> *It is OK, don't be ashamed,*
> *not many can hear*
> *and feel the way that you do.*
> *You have learned to listen to us.*
> *The wind speaks to you*
> *and the flowers call your name.*
> *Here in our land, magic is real.*
> *However, not like the magic*
> *you see on TV or read in your books.*
> *The real magic is of the heart*
> *not spells in books.*
> *Walk through the path of the garden.*
> *I will light your way."*

Violet's heart filled with joy and excitement, yet she was still hesitant. An inner voice told her to listen to the moon. The breeze began to billow through the tall grass and blowing through the top of the trees, her coat flowing behind her as she embarked on a journey. As she walked through the grass, she placed one barefoot in front of the other. She could feel the chilly blades of grass beneath her feet as she walked on and on, for what seemed like five miles instead of only one. Maybe it was the mystery of the shadows that made the path seem longer than it actually was.

Finally she came to a tree that was lit perfectly by the waterfall in the moonlight. There in the middle of this tall tree was a secret door, a portal to another world. It was a sight to see – absolutely breathtaking. Above the portal on the tree was a sign with the words:

"WELCOME. ENTER IF YOU BELIEVE."

Her hands started to tremble, not from fear, rather from the excitement of the unknown. Violet grasped the handle to the door and whispered *"I believe,"* just like she did when she was a small child.

As she walked through the door, Violet shrunk, smaller and smaller with each step. Once through the door, she saw a tunnel of light before her. She started down the curvy path, and walked until she came to a halting stop. There were two paths ahead with signs pointing in different directions.

On one sign were the words:

← FAIRYLAND THIS WAY

And on the other, with an arrow pointing right were the words:

If you are afraid, exit to the right. →

Without a second thought, Violet chose the path to the left – into Fairyland.

Once Violet ventured on the path to Fairyland, she strolled through the forest, as the light from sunset began to shine brightly through the trees. The forest was full of beautiful flowers, more vibrant than any color in the rainbow. There were hundreds of dragonflies and butterflies fluttering about. Violet heard the sound of birds chirping a song. She could also hear the sound of frogs croaking as they jumped from lily pad to lily pad. As she listened to the sound of a waterfall in the distance, Violet heard a voice that sounded like an angel singing. She quickly looked around to see where the voice came from. There, next to the path, stood a shimmering fairy.

"With love and light
fairies will be within sight,
with intentions so true,
your dreams can come true.
Fairies will dance in the moonlight
and sing beautifully tonight."

"I'm Annabelle," said the owner of the voice, as she spread wide her white, shimmering wings.

Violet extended her hand, "Nice to meet you, I'm Violet."

"I'm so happy you believe in us," Annabelle said, cupping Violets hand with her left. "Connecting with you is important for us, as well as for you. You are like all of us too, for love and light is within you."

Violet was amazed beyond belief to be in such a magical place, it looked like something from her dreams, or like her imagination and visions when she read her books. This, however, felt more real than anything she had ever felt. Annabelle's eyes were so blue, they were the color of the deep blue water that shimmered below her feet. Violet saw love, compassion, and a fire from deep within Annabelle's soul.

Looking into those beautiful eyes, Violet had the thought '*She has the heart of gold and the strength and courage of a lioness*!'

Golden blonde hair draped past Annabelle's shoulders, like a waterfall flowing over a creek. Annabelle moved from the path and sat on a large rock by the water. Her dress was the same color as her wings, with jewels that covered the bodice – a dress truly fit for a fairy goddess.

Upon her head sat a halo of white roses and baby's breath. Her skin was so light – flawless – and she wore no makeup, however her face radiated pure, natural beauty. A golden light followed her wherever she went – as if the sun were a backdrop set up for her portrait.

The sun set and the moon began to rise higher and higher, as the sun faded into the darkness.

"Walk with me," Annabelle said.

Violet followed behind her as Annabelle began to walk along the moonlit path in the middle of the Fairyland forest. The sound of the waterfall grew closer and closer until Annabelle stopped. The sight before them was a waterfall like no other. It was glowing blue, like magic with sparkling stars, as the moonlight kissed the waters. The music of the birds began to chirp, followed by the croaking and splashing of frogs.

The dragonflies and butterflies were sitting by the water, as if waiting for something.

Annabelle stood on the largest stepping stone then another fairy followed, and then another and another, until the creek was surrounded by dancing fairies. Violet just watched while the moonlight and fairies danced across the water – as though the element of water and the fairies were one. It was the most beautiful sight she had ever seen and the most gorgeous song she had ever heard.

After the fairies finished dancing to the sweetest, most captivating music her ears ever had the privilege to hear, Violet sat there in wonder and was full of admiration for this enchanting moment.

"That was beautiful," Violet said.

"Thank you," another voice said.

"You're very welcome," Violet replied, as she looked around to see who this new voice belonged to.

"My name is Christina," the fairy said, as she held out her hand and Violet reached to shake it. Christina then wrapped her arms around Violet in a warm embrace.

"Welcome to Fairyland. I have a feeling we will be great friends, I can feel it," Christina said.

"OK," replied Violet, feeling a little awkward.

"Well I will see you around soon," Christina said, as she turned to walk away.

Violet watched as this beautiful girl, who was a little older than herself, walked into the forest. Christina would probably be like a sophomore in college, if she were in the mortal world. Christina's dress was a gorgeous orange color like a Carolina Lily; it was long and elegant and had beading perfectly spaced along the front. '*Tomorrow will be a new day, now it is time to go home*,' Violet said to herself

"Violet," Annabelle called, breaking into Violet's thoughts.

"Ma'am?" Violet questioned, as she turned to face Annabelle.

"You can rest here in Fairyland, you don't have to go home now, if you don't want to. Time in Fairyland is very different from the mortal world. Days here can be like minutes or hours in your world." Annabelle explained.

"Really? That is amazing, where should I go to rest? I'm very tired; this is a lot to take in." Violet said with a yawn.

"Yes it is. I will take you to a place, so you can rest and re-energize."

Annabelle and Violet walked through the forest as the fireflies, moon and a thousand stars lit their way.

They arrived at a garden, filled with hundreds of different varieties of flowers. The flowers here grew even more wildly than those in the garden path at home.

"Here you are," Annabelle pointed to a beautiful violet flower. "Climb upon the toadstool and rest in the flower as if you were sleeping in your own bed."

Violet stepped up on the toadstool and climbed into the flower. The center was so soft it was like velvet. The petals were so silky and soft to the touch. Annabelle covered her up with an extra flower petal to keep her warm, like a mother tucking her child into bed.

"Sleep well and rest awhile, for you have a big day tomorrow," Annabelle said, as she flew off into the night.

Violet drifted off to sleep, the flower was so comfortable and the moon, as always, sang her a sweet lullaby.

Chapter 2

The Fairyland Queen

"Wake up sleepyhead!" exclaimed Christina.

Violet woke up rubbing her eyes, as she opened them she saw Christina smiling at her with a smile like sunshine. Christina's eyes were brown and she was beautiful with dark skin and a pixie style haircut.

"I'm up," replied Violet, still yawning.

"Well lets go!" Christina shouted excitedly as she pulled Violet off the flower onto the toadstool and then onto the ground.

"OK! OK! What's going on?" Violet asked.

"Well we have some things to do today," Christina replied.

"Like what kind of things?" Violet asked.

"You'll see," Christina said, playfully taunting her new friend.

Violet stood there staring at her friend completely confused, yet up for whatever Christina had in store.

Christina led Violet to a garden, a secret garden that very few knew about. They passed the magic waterfall, the large flowers, then through the path of toadstools. They walked through a cave of crystals and jewels. There were sapphires, amethyst, rubies, emeralds and every other crystal you could think of. They covered the walls of the cave from the bottom to the top. The sun was shining so bright that every crystal sparkled like stars in the sky. The path to their destination was about a mile long.

Standing in front of them at their destination was a huge silver gate, covered with scroll designs of flowers. Jewels were placed in the center of each flower. Christina lifted the latch using her right hand and she pushed open the gate. Beyond the gate was even more of a spectacular view than the garden that Violet slept in. There were more flowers and plants. The colors where even more vibrant and magical.

Christina led her to a rose, where they climbed on toadstool like steps that led them to a white rose. Inside the flower was Annabelle.

"I believe you two have met before," Christina said jokingly.

"Good morning, Violet. You look well rested," Annabelle said.

"Yes ma'am, thank you." replied Violet.

"You don't have to call me ma'am. Annabelle will suit just fine."

"OK, Annabelle it is," Violet said with a smile.

"Violet, I would like you to meet the Queen, Mother of the fairies, in a not so formal setting," said Annabelle, as a fairy with iridescent wings slowly landed inside the rose. Her hair was blonde like Annabelle's. She had emerald green eyes, that sweetly peered into Violet's. A silver crown of flowers like the flowers on the gate that led them here.

"Hello, Violet," the Queen said.

"Hello, it is an honor to meet you," replied Violet as she bowed down to the Queen.

"You can call me Cassandra. Let's have a seat and enjoy some tea and cupcakes."

Violet took a seat upon the flower, as did Christina, Queen Cassandra and Annabelle.

Sitting in front of them were teacups made from tiny acorns. The teapot was made of a larger acorn with a flower stem for the handle. The sight before Violet was absolutely beyond any magic in any fairy tale book or movie. The Queen then picked up the teapot and poured tea into all the teacups. Small beings flew nearby, as they got closer Violet realized that they were small fairies, and they brought them cupcakes.

"Here are these special cupcakes for you, we made them with love," said a small blue winged fairy.

"Thank you very much, Maddy, they look amazing. I love strawberry cupcakes with heart crystals. They are my favorite," said the Queen.

"You are very welcome, Queen Cassandra." said the little blue fairy as she flew away.

"Well Violet, what do you think of Fairyland?" the Queen asked, as she took a sip of her tea and anxiously waited for Violet's answer.

The three sat and talked about Violet's experience, in between sipping tea and eating cupcakes. The garden was filled with laughter of all three fairies, as Violet remained in shock at everything she had seen.

"Well I would like to speak with you about your journey here. You are here for a reason you cannot know yet as your mind is not ready to accept all that will later be known to you. There is much to learn about Fairyland and about yourself. This is not so much a journey, like traveling, rather its a journey within your heart. You are beautiful and capable of so much more than you ever thought possible."

"Like what?" Violet asked politely, feeling a bit anxious.

"You will just have to wait and see," Queen Cassandra said with a smile.

"Oh, OK," replied Violet, in a disappointed voice.

"Don't stress about it sweetie, it will happen in time." said Cassandra, reassuringly.

Christina nodded her head in assurance "I will take good care of her," she said to the Queen.

"I know you will. So let's see what is next," the Queen said.

"Oh yes," Christina agreed.

"I will let you do your thing," Annabelle said, as she flew away.

"Violet, please stand up and turn around," Queen Cassandra requested, as she took her wand from her bag.

The wand was made from the hawthorn tree. Attached to the top of the wand was a heart shaped cutout and inside the carved heart sat a rose quartz crystal sphere.

The elves handmade the wand for Queen Cassandra. They make a new wand every time a fairy princess is named the new Queen of Fairyland.

Cassandra waved her wand in circles, as the crystal began glowing, out poured what looked like a million tiny swirling stars. They wrapped themselves around Violet, embracing her as if she and the stars were one. Violet could see the magic and felt the tingles surrounding her – as her coat transformed into a dress. The dress was purple with a V neck. A ribbon with purple and white flowers was tied around her waist. A white, sheer fabric that was connected in the middle by an amethyst crystal heart pendant had been draped over her purple dress. The sheer fabric was open, accept for the pendent and the long whimsical sleeves. Upon her head set a halo of baby's breath. Violet looked and felt like a fairy without wings.

Looking Violet up and down to admire her handy work, Cassandra said, "You look stunning. I will leave the two of you." the Queen said to them as she disappeared in a beam of light.

"Wow you look amazing! How do you feel?" Christina said.

"Amazing! I feel like a fairy, however that feels," Violet replied.

"Let me show you why you feel the way you do," Christina said as she led Violet to the base of the magic waterfall. Violet looked into the pool and instantly smiled at her reflection. She had to admit she looked gorgeous with her new dress and halo.

"Now I look like one of you!" Violet exclaimed.

"You sure do!" said Christina.

"Thank you," Violet replied.

"I want to show you something very special," Christina said.

"What is it?" asked Violet.

"Follow me," Christina replied, as she turned to the path.

Christina led Violet to a very special place that was known as Dragon Island. They walked through a dark cave until they saw light at the other end. Once they reached the light at the end of the cave, they stepped out into a small clearing and looked up. What a view it was! There were many dragons soaring about through the sky! Violet stood there in awe of this magnificent place and the gorgeous dragons.

Christina led Violet to a place within Dragon Island called Crystal Corner. Hidden behind a large quartz crystal was a beautiful white dragon, almost invisible, as if it was camouflaged by the crystal.

"Wow! She's gorgeous," Violet said in awe, as she walked toward the resting dragon.

"She is," Christina agreed.

Violet placed her hand on the dragon's head, and a ton of memories came flooding back in a flash. Violet remembered her dreams of riding on a dragon and flying through clouds.

When Violet was around five years old, she decided to climb out the top window from her two story house. She thought that she could fly like the fairies did in her books and movies. Just as she jumped, something caught her and broke her fall. It was Mystic, her imaginary dream dragon. All her life, Violet had thought this was only a dream; now she knew it was all real.

When Violet was ten years old a man broke into the house while everyone was asleep. He rummaged through the place and headed up the stairs. Something pushed him down the stairs and he tumbled to the floor.

Objects began flying at him whenever he stood back up to try to go up again. After the man went running for his life, the dragon came into view. Mystic headed up the stairs to check on Violet, where she found Violet still fast asleep.

Anytime there was danger, Mystic had been there to protect her. Violet remembered those purple eyes and loving nature. The moment that she looked into Mystic's eyes, she realized that Mystic must be her guardian.

"Violet, Mystic is your guardian," Christina said.

"I remember her, but why?" Violet asked.

"I can't say, because I don't know everything," Christina replied.

"What do you know?" Violet asked.

"That's it – just that she is your guardian." Christina answered. "I knew Mystic would show you memories because she asked me to bring you."

"She did?" asked Violet, as she looked at Mystic and waited for an answer. Mystic nodded her head in confirmation.

"Let's go for a ride, hop on Mystic," Christina said and they climbed up on the dragon. They took off flying through the air. It felt familiar, like it did in her dreams, however this was even better. Mystic flew all over Dragon Island, over a large body of water, and landed in a lagoon surrounded by sand.

"Here we are," Christina said.

"Wow! Where is here?" Violet asked.

"Mermaid Lagoon, of course," she said.

"Seriously?" Violet asked in disbelief.

"Yes. Meet Isabelle," Christina said as a beautiful woman surfaced the water. She had long sparkling midnight blue hair that draped down to the small of her back; she had emerald green eyes and fair skin. Isabelle swam over to a rock where she climbed up to take a seat. The waves began crashing into the rock keeping her fin moist with the salt water.

"Hello, I'm Violet."

"Nice to meet you," Isabelle said.

"Wow this is beautiful; the water is so clear and blue. It is nothing like the water in the mortal world." Violet said.

"Yes it is beautiful here. People are destroying Earth in the mortal world. If people wouldn't pollute the water by littering in it, and discarding chemicals into the water sources, then they, too, would have healthy water. See, the pollution is like poison to us, the animals, and anyone who uses water to survive. Everyone needs to recycle what they can to help Earth and better the planet for everyone. They should start using more natural things that the Earth has given them. Come with me and I will show you what I mean." Isabelle said.

"How are we supposed to swim? We don't have fins." Violet asked.

"Like this," Isabelle said as she raised her right hand and blew fairy dust their way. Violet's feet morphed into a silver fin, Christina's feet shifted into a fin of orange and pink. They jumped in and began swimming through the deep water, passing schools of fish, colorful reefs and corals along the way. They stopped at the wall that separated the mortal world, and its pollution, from Fairyland.

"Look over the wall and you will see what I mean," Isabelle said.

Violet and Christina both looked over the wall and suddenly felt sick. There really was no water, just trash floating in an oily substance. It was a horrible sight to see and it smelled awful.

"Oh my!" Violet exclaimed, shocked.

"Yes Violet, we had to put a wall of magic up to protect Fairyland from the pollution as much as we can. We have trolls and elves that help us every day to keep this land clean and beautiful. It would be easier if the mortal world helped. They don't understand that what they do affects us in Fairyland, themselves and every other being on the planet."

After swimming back to Mystic, Isabelle made their fins vanish, so they could walk on land. As she climbed upon Mystic, the magnitude of the damage humans are doing to Earth hit her. Violet sat on Mystic and started crying as she hugged her guardian. It hurt her to know all of this and it broke her heart to see it.

Violet looked at Isabelle, tears streaming down her face, "It was nice to meet you Isabelle, I'm sorry for what has been done."

"Oh sweetie it is not your fault," Isabelle replied.

"I'm not completely innocent," Violet said.

"I know sweetie. However, education is key. Now that you know, I know that you will help make it better, even if it is one person at a time. Take care; I hope to see you again," Isabelle said as she waved goodbye for now and swam away into deeper water.

Violet and Christina flew back over the land to Dragon Island and Crystal Corner. They left Mystic behind her crystal, then headed back to the garden to take a nap and think and process everything.

After their nap, Violet and Christina went for a walk to the secret garden at the edge of the dark forest.

Christina explained to Violet, "Do not go past the edge of the garden because the Dark Forest is where evil and darkness lurks. As long as you don't cross out of the garden, you will be safe. Although the Sorcerer can't cross through, we have had some fairies, trolls and elves disappear over the years. I guess they didn't heed the warnings."

Chapter 3

Edge Of The Dark Forest

Christina and Violet were playing in the secret garden on the edge of the dark forest.

"Hey Violet, I need to run," said Christina.

"OK. I'm going to hang around here and relax awhile," replied Violet.

Christina gave her friend a hug and took off through the forest.

Violet began humming a tune of joy and dancing in circles; she smiled and began laughing because she was full of so much joy. As she basked in the rays of the sun and the breeze, her dress billowed in the wind. Violet twirled around and around in her new dress, enjoying the way it swished and billowed around her legs. Violet spun into a man on her last turn.

"I'm so sorry," she said apologetically.

"It's OK, Beautiful, I don't mind. What is your name?" the man asked, smiling.

"Violet, like the flower," she said blushing.

"Hello, Violet, like the flower. A Beautiful name, and very fitting for someone with a smile and beauty like yours," he said.

"Well thank you," replied Violet as her cheeks turned a deeper shade of pink.

"My name is Merin," he said with a sexy seductive voice.

Violet looked down shyly, as this gorgeous man stood before her. Merin was tall and strong with short spiky hair that was black as night. His hand reached to cup her chin between his left thumb and forefinger. He then raised her head to the level of his eyes.

"There now that is better, never look to the ground, you are too damn beautiful not to be seen." Merin said as he lifted her chin up so that he could see her eyes. Violet looked up and into the electric blue windows to his soul. Those eyes were absolutely mesmerizing and she felt as if she was put in a trance, she felt as if she could stare into his eyes forever. As if Merin could sense her fear and hesitation, he grabbed hold of her hand and she snapped back to reality.

"I will never hurt you or your beautiful heart," he said sincerely.

Violet did not know how to react to Merins charming ways. "I have to go, it was nice to meet you!" she exclaimed.

"Can I see you again?" asked Merin, not letting go her hand.

"Umm, I don't know," she said shyly.

"Well how about tomorrow, when the sun rises?" He asked feeling hopeful.

"OK," she said, as she pulled away her hand and quickly vanished from his sight.

One look into Violet's eyes and Merin was lost within the depths of her very soul. She looked at him like no one ever had before. It was like she could see into his soul and they were connected. Merin felt her heart and how pure it was; it was love at first sight.

Merin couldn't believe what he was feeling. He was the son and apprentice to an evil sorcerer from the Dark Forest. He had a dark past, because he walked in the shadow of his father.

All he had ever known was darkness, he had never really known anything else. He felt he did not deserve her.

Merin kept asking himself, "What the hell just happened? What. Just. Happened. To. Me?"

Chapter 4

Betrayal

Zane and King Andrew were the best of friends and they were practically inseparable. As his faithful knight, Zane was completely trusted by the King. The King had always told Zane that he trusted him with his life.

Zane, on the other hand, envied everything his friend had – money, the Queen and the fact that he was royal.

One day he and the king went for a stroll where the sunlight and moonlight could never touch – The Dark Forest. The king was talking with Zane and contemplating what to do with this part of Fairyland. The King felt it had been vacant far too long and it was time for a positive change.

Zane began hearing voices that told him to come and visit again – without the king and to keep it a secret, for he may soon have everything he ever wanted.

The very next day Zane told King Andrew he had something to do and that he would be back in time for the dance. He walked out the doors of the castle and headed toward the location, as instructed by the voices he was listening to. Zane left discretely – in stepping over the edge from the light to the dark side, he would be forever changed.

"Come and take a sample from the pond and pour it in the king's drink. Once you do this, the king will die silently, then you will be named king. You will have everything you have ever wanted and more," said the voice.

Zane took off his necklace, that held a vile of fairy dust; he emptied and rinsed it out. He dipped it in the water to fill it up with poison and he placed the lid on it. Zane put the chain back around his neck, and he tucked it under his armor. He stood up and walked out of the Dark Forest and back into Fairyland to the castle. As he turned toward the castle, Zane felt a sliver of guilt for what he was about to do. Yet the rest of him was consumed with envy to the point where he would stop at nothing to get what he wanted, even when it meant killing his life-long best friend.

The King trusted him and he never questioned Zane. "Would you like some wine sir?" Zane asked.

"Sure, would you bring a glass for the Queen as well?" King Andrew requested.

"Of course, it will be my pleasure." Zane replied, flashing a sinister grin.

Zane walked over to the table with the wine, and looked around to make sure that no one was watching. He took the bottle of Dark Forest liquid from around his neck, and poured the contents into the King's cup. He held the cup in his right hand, and held a cup of just wine in his left for the Queen.

Everyone in Fairyland was gathered in the gardens to celebrate the Summer Solstice. All the fairies, elves and trolls were dancing the night away and were having an amazing time. The king started to struggle to keep his balance while dancing with his Queen. King Andrew began to feel sick and weak. He told everyone that he was not feeling well and that he would be turning in for the night. The dance was instantly over and everyone left, as Cassandra helped King Andrew to his bed. She left him there to rest and went to make her own preparations for bed.

The Queen was exhausted and wanted to relax in a bath. She soaked in the tub for awhile, surrounded by candlelight. The aroma of lavender and vanilla filled the air. It always calmed her, and helped her to get a good night's sleep.

She got out of the tub and covered her body with a pink silk gown and went to check on her King as he rested. As she reached his bed, she realized that he was not breathing. She laid her ear to his chest, listening for a heartbeat, there was no sound coming from his chest. The only sound she could hear was her own sobbing and her heart breaking. Her king, her love was dead.

The Queen cried out for help. The guards came running at her call, seeing her sobbing by the bed, they ran to her side to see if they could help. It was too late. Their beloved King Andrew was dead.

The next day the kingdom had to prepare for King Andrew's unexpected funeral. Sadness filled Fairyland that day. The Queen was crying in her room and Zane ran to her side to comfort her in her time of sorrow.

"I'm sorry my Queen," he said as he pulled her chin up to look into her eyes. Tears started to well up in her eyes, so he hugged her tightly as he inhaled the floral essence of her hair.

'*She will be mine,*' he thought to himself. The king had long ago requested that Zane would replace him as king if anything were to happen. Zane kissed the Queen on her cheek and left the room.

King Andrew was laid on a large leaf in the middle of Fairyland, so that every creature, which included the mermaids and the dragons, could pay their final respects, and place a flower in the circle around his body.

The Fairy tradition of placing flowers around the body represents the sacred circle of eternal life. The fairies believed that when they created a circle with flowers from the fairy garden, those they have lost will in someway come back to them. This was their way of not saying goodbye, rather of saying, "See you in another life." The Queen was the last one to lay her flower down, closing the sacred circle of eternal life.

"I will see you again, my love" she whispered in his ear, then kissed his cold lips. The Queen Cassandra, sobbing uncontrollably, was escorted back to the castle to continue life without her king.

Only a few weeks after saying goodbye to the king, Zane sneaked into the Queens room while she was sleeping. Quietly unbuttoning his shirt and unzipping his pants, he quickly removed all his clothes. He slipped in between the satin sheets. The Queen was in a deep sleep with tear stains upon her face. Zane placed his hands gently on her cheek to brush away a strand of hair. He grabbed a hold of her head and pulled her toward him. Half asleep the Queen moved closer and they kissed, he ran his hand down her back as if he was about to make love to her. The Queen felt something was not right and woke up with a start.

"Help!" she yelled.

"My love, my Queen, I love and care for you," Zane exclaimed, as he struggled to get dressed.

"I doubt it and I'm not your Queen," she said as she slapped him across his face. Hearing her cries, the guards burst through the double doors, anxious to learn what was harming their queen. Seeing Zane struggling with his clothes, they immediately surrounded him and faced the queen, awaiting instructions.

"Apprehend him! I banish him from these premises," she cried in anger.

"But my Queen, he is to be king," the Captain of the Guard replied, astonished at the sudden turn of events.

"I don't care, if I can't have my King Andrew, there will be no king, only me, the Queen. I will rule for the both of us. Zane how could you? He trusted you with his life!" the Queen said.

"Yes ma'am! He wanted me to take care of you always," Zane replied.

"It didn't mean take care of me in bed!" she yelled, "I would not doubt that you had something to do with his death! You were always envious of everything he had." Then to the guards, "Remove him from my sight!"

The guards picked Zane up and carried him out of the castle, past the gardens and to the edge of the Dark Forest. After pushing him into the trees, the guards put a force shield up so that Zane could never again return to Fairyland.

Much time passed as Zane figured out what to do next. Deciding he needed his own castle, he convinced the trolls of the Dark Forest to help him. Together they built a castle from trees and stones found on the forest floor.

One day, the voice that guided him to give Andrew the poison, just disappeared. Even though he was very angry that nothing had gone as planned, Zane still needed *that* voice to help him get revenge.

Eventually, Zane realized that the voice was just the demon inside him, just like a devil on your shoulder. Once his castle was built and everything was in place, Zane sat by the pond of poison contemplating what to do next.

One day something strange happened — a mirror opened in the ripple and showed an image of him— or was it? It looked like him yet different, this man wore a black cloak and in his hands he held a staff. On the top of the staff was a dragon's claw, holding a crystal ball. Startled, Zane looked away when he heard a sound of someone walking at the edge of the Dark Forest.

Walking over to see who it was, Zane felt heavier with every step he took. He realized he was wearing a black cloak and in his right hand a staff appeared – just like the image in the mirror from the pond.

Peering around a tree at the edge of the forest into Fairyland, he saw a beautiful fairy with long hair, the color of fire.

"Hello," Zane said.

"Hello," a woman's voice replied, looking around to see from whence the voice came.

"Would you come closer so I can see you more clearly," Zane asked, stepping into a clearing in the forest.

With some hesitation, she took a few steps toward the edge of the Dark Forest.

"Come closer, so I can see all of your beauty?" he said, using his most seductive voice.

"Of course," she said blushing as she took the steps across the edge into the darkness. My name is Phoenix." she said.

"And I'm in love," replied Zane, looking directly into her eyes.

"Oh stop it." she said smiling.

"I'm serious, nothing could compare to your beauty." he said.

"Thank you," she said, dreamily.

"So would you like to have dinner with me, I bet you're hungry?" asked Zane.

"Sure. I could eat something," she said.

Zane led her into his domain where he flattered and fed her. After dinner Zane stared deeply into her eyes, caressed her body and kissed her deeply. Phoenix was intrigued by this sexy man, and oh, she wanted him as badly as he craved her. He untied the corset wrapped around her body and her dress dropped to the floor. He gripped her fiery red hair tight and pulled her head back so that her neck was visible for him to kiss. His lips lightly touched her skin and then he opened his mouth as if he is going to suck, however, he bit down. Phoenix moaned as she was in complete ecstasy, she felt hot and completely intoxicated by this man. Zane swept her up and carried her to his bed, where they made wild love for three days.

The morning after the third day Phoenix started to feel sick. Zane rushed to her side "What is wrong, my beauty?" he asked.

"I don't feel well," she said.

"Maybe you need food. Or more love," he said jokingly.

"You're right, maybe food will help, "she replied weakly.

Zane had the trolls bring her some fruit and some bread rolls, but it was no use, because she threw it up instantly.

"I believe I'm pregnant," she fearfully.

"Are you serious?" he asked.

"That is the only explanation for the way I've been feeling," she said.

Months went by until the day their son Merin was born. Phoenix was not in labor long before Merin arrived. The trolls delivered their baby with no problems. The midwife troll handed the baby boy to his mother and left the room.

"Look honey, he is handsome," she said.

"Yes he is," Zane replied.

"We shall call him Merin," she said, admiring her handsome baby boy.

"So what shall his middle name be? What is your birth name?"

"Zane."

Phoenix's mouth dropped; she was frightened and wondered what she had done.

She thought Zane would be an old man, not this handsome man before her.

"How did I not know this before? I feel like I've been under a spell," she said.

"You have. You've have been under my love spell," Zane replied with a grin.

"Well hello, Zane." she said, shaking.

Phoenix was frightened. She began to wonder how she could escape with Merin. This is not where she wanted her son to grow up.

She was thinking, '*This evil man will not be a part of Merin's upbringing*.' She didn't know Zane could hear her thoughts.

Listening to her thoughts, he realized that he had to stop her. He did not know the spell would wear off when she gave birth.

'*I have to stop her leaving. Merin is my connection to the rest of Fairyland*,' he thought to himself. '*This child can bring me whatever I want or desire. I will have my own personal slave and apprentice*.' With that thought, Zane ripped Merin from his mother's arms. Zane grabbed his staff and before she could protest, turned Phoenix to stone. There was no way he was going to allow her to take away his chance of getting revenge on the fairies.

As Merin grew up, Zane taught him invisibility so that he could cross the edge and abduct fairies to brainwash them. Once brought over the edge they were told Zane was their king and to stay away from the other side. Merin did this for many years, just as his father had asked of him – until one day he stopped.

On his sixteenth birthday, Merin eventually started to think for himself and talked to the fairies. Listening to the fairies, he began hearing stories about how evil his father was, and the rumors that he had killed the king. Hearing these stories, Merin realized he had been lied to his whole life.

Zane, his father, was evil and it is rumored the Queen believed that he killed their king so many years ago, and how she had banished Zane from Fairyland. Now Merin understood the reason his father could not cross the edge. Merin decided to take his dragon and leave the forest never to return. He flew to Dragon Island, where he rested in a cave that he eventually called home. He knew that once Zane learned of the betrayal, he would find a way to make Merin pay.

Life isn't about
Waiting
for the storm
to pass...
It's about learning
to dance
in the Rain!

-Vivian Greene

Chapter 5

Dancing In The Rain

Violet woke up stunned at all that she had learned yesterday. The sun was starting to rise through the trees, and she realized that it was time to meet Merin. When Violet arrived, Merin was waiting for her, a flower held behind his back. He approached, got down on one knee, took the golden daisy from behind his back and handed it to her.

"A beautiful flower of sunshine for a smile so bright, yet 'tis nothing, compared to your beauty."

"Thank you," Violet said, blushing, as she took the daisy from his hand.

"You look quite a bit different today than yesterday."

"Oh yea, this dress was made for me by the Queen," Violet replied, swirling around so the dress swished and billowed around her ankles.

"Wow! it truly is stunning and suits you well."

"Thank you," she said, smiling.

"Shall we?" Merin said as he held out his arm to her.

Violet wrapped her arm around his and they began to walk.

"So, what brings you to Fairyland, Beautiful?"

"Well I'm not really sure, apparently I'm on a journey."

"Ah. What do you think of Fairyland so far?" Merin inquired.

"It is absolutely breathtaking and amazing – so magical and friendly," Violet replied, eyes shining at the wonder of it all.

"Well that is wonderful. I'm glad you like it."

"I don't like it, I love it! I feel so at home here, unlike the mortal world, where I have never felt at home," she exclaimed.

"I hear there are a lot of horrible things there, in the mortal world," he said, as he guided Violet around a mud puddle in the middle of the path.

"Well, yeah, there are terrible things in the mortal world. Some people have huge hearts and help out when they can, while others destroy the world with darkness and with weapons. There is killing and kidnapping on the news all the time. There are also weapons that are not visible, yet can cause so much pain. Humans use words as weapons to hurt each other, too. In the mortal world, people judge you for being different in any way that they don't agree with. They don't believe in magic, or anything for that matter. They only believe in what they see."

"I'm so sorry. I'm glad you are here and are safe," Merin said.

"Yeah, I'm here for now, not sure what is going to happen for me here. I'm excited and scared at the same time," she said.

"Don't be scared, I will protect you," Merin said, laying his hand protectively over hers, where it lay on his arm.

"Thank you. I'm not so scared of Fairyland, rather the idea of not knowing what to expect."

"Well isn't that the beauty of life sometimes, always surprises and never knowing what the day has in store. Here we are," he said.

They arrived in a garden by a creek, no one else was around, they were alone. Merin grabbed hold of Violet's hand as he walked over to a basket he had set on the grass, in the shade of a willow tree. He took a seat while still holding Violets hand and pulled her down with him, so that she landed on his lap.

"Well hello, Beautiful," he said as he stared into her eyes, thinking, ' *A man could get lost in those depths.*

"Hi," Violet said, blushing.

Merin placed his right palm on her face and pulled her forward as he placed his lips on hers and they embraced in the sweetest kiss she had ever had, yet it was brief. Merin stopped, pulled away and kissed her on her cheek. He continued to smile.

"Are you hungry?"

"Sure," Violet replied.

"Here you are," he said as he pulled out a bowl of fruit and berries.

"Mmm. Strawberries are my favorite."

"Mine too," Merin replied.

Merin picked up a strawberry to feed it to Violet. She opened her mouth as the fruit came closer to her lips, she bit down. The juices that flowed through her mouth were so juicy and sweet. Violet picked up a strawberry to feed to Merin. He opened his mouth to taste the sweet fruit from her hands.

'*Wow they are good and they taste even better with her feeding me,*' he thought to himself. He chewed and swallowed it and then fed Violet another, and she in turn fed him one more. Merin kissed her again, and pulled back so he could see her eyes.

"The strawberries taste even better on your lips," he said.

"They do?"

"Oh yes. See, the strawberry juices blended with your sweetness is the perfect and most delicious thing my tongue has ever tasted."

"Wow," Violet said softly. It was the only word she could get out, as his words and presence had rendered her speechless.

"Would you like something to drink?" he asked, as he handed her a silver goblet filled with water. She took a few sips to wash down the food.

"Merin?" she said.

"Yes, Beautiful?" he replied, a questioning lilt to his voice.

"This day has been amazing and I have really enjoyed it. It looks like it is about to rain, the clouds are getting dark and heavy," she said.

"Really? I had not even noticed. I was so busy being lost with you."

"And I you," she said.

"Just because it is going to rain does not mean that our day has to end," he said.

"Oh? What do you suggest?" she asked, smiling.

The clouds began to thicken and rain began to pour down from the sky. Merin stood up, grabbed Violet's hand to help her to her feet. They ran towards the creek.

"Follow me," he said.

Merin stepped on a stone in the creek and Violet followed as he hopped from one stone to the next. After a short distance, he stopped and turned around to face her. He pulled her closer by her waist and started leading her in a dance. They danced to the sound of raindrops hitting the creek, like a secret drum. As water hit the stones, each droplet made a different sound, a different note. They danced in the rain for what would be hours in the mortal world. Merin twirled Violet in circles as they danced their own secret dance.

"You are so beautiful. As the water runs down your face, all I can think about is kissing you," he said, as his heart skipped a beat.

"I feel so different," she replied.

"Because you are. You are dancing happily in something you were going to run away from," he said.

"Yeah, I guess you're right," she said smiling.

"Lets lay down and dry off," Merin said

"How can we dry off when its raining?" she asked.

"Watch!"

As soon as he said that, the sun came out. He picked her up and placed her on solid ground. He laid her down on the grass softly and he lay down next to her. A beautiful rainbow crossed the sky as the colors transformed from gray to blue.

"I've never seen anything so beautiful."

"After every storm, there is always something beautiful that happens, just like this rainbow," Merin explained.

"It's amazing! You know, I've always wondered whether there was a pot of gold at the end of the rainbow, just like they tell in stories."

"Of course there is. Every myth has some sort of truth," Merin replied. "How do you think they came to be? Leprechauns do protect the pot of gold when the rainbow appears, for fear someone will try and steal it. The rainbow is like the treasure map with an X that marks the spot.

"How do you know this?"

"Because the Leprechauns are my friends," Merin replied, a twinkle in his eyes.

"That is pretty awesome!"

"Yeah, it is. They're interesting creatures."

"So, may I ask, what kind of creature are you?"

"I'm half elf and half fairy. Unfortunately I never knew my mother. She was a fairy. I was raised by my father, the elf."

Merin and Violet lay there drying, as the sun began to set. The birds ended their song and the frogs and crickets started theirs. The moon started peaking through the clouds.

"I love the moon." Violet said in a soft, dreamy voice. "Isn't she beautiful?"

"Yes she is."

"I love staring at the moon and stars. There are not any stars visible tonight," Violet said, sadly.

"Watch," he said as he waved his hands like he was separating the clouds and then they disappeared like magic, displaying the thousands of stars surrounding the Milky Way.

"How did you do that?" she asked.

"Magic," he replied with a grin.

"I've always wanted to touch the stars," she said, dreamily.

"Hmm. Maybe you can," he said.

"How?' Violet asked in disbelief.

"You will see on our next date," he said.

"Oh, so you think there will be another date?" she asked, teasing him.

"Of course . . . well at least I hope so, Beautiful," he stared at her with hope in his eyes. "I hope you wish to have another date. If your answer is yes, meet me here tomorrow, after the sun has set.

"OK," replied Violet.

Merin stood up and pulled Violet to her feet, and into his arms. Arms tight around her waist, he spun in circles, not letting her go. He placed her back on the ground to kiss her.

"You are even more gorgeous in the moonlight. I will see you tomorrow, Beautiful," he said.

Violet placed a quick kiss on his lips and turned to walk away. Merin appeared in front of her, just for another long sweet kiss goodnight. He then disappeared into the night and Violet walked back to her resting flower, smiling ear to ear.

Chapter 6

Magik

Violet woke up with the sun kissing her face.

"So what happened yesterday?" Christina asked pouncing on the petals of the flower.

"Nothing much," Violet said smiling.

"You better spill," Christina said.

Violet got up and walked with Christina through the forest as she explained to her all that happened yesterday. "I'm meeting him tonight at sundown. I can't wait!" Violet said excitedly.

"Wow that sounds lovely," Christina said.

"Oh, yes, it was," Violet replied, dreamily. "I can't wait to see him again."

With a twinkle in her eyes, Christina said, "Its good you are not seeing him until later. This morning you are ours!"

"Sounds good, what are we doing?"

"Let's get going, we are to meet Annabelle in the large fairy garden," Christina replied

Violet followed Christina past the sunflowers and into the fairy play land. It looked like an amusement park made out of flowers, fallen trees, and things that were just a part of the earth.

"Hey Violet!" Annabelle called.

"Hey," Violet said as Annabelle arrived by her side and embraced her in a hug.

"One thing that fairies love to do is play and let go of whatever is on their mind." She said as she ran for the see-saw, Violet and Christina following. Christina sat in the middle, Violet and Annabelle set on the ends. The see-saw was made of a fallen tree, with thin cuts of the tree stump as for seats.

"Hey lets go slide," Christina said.

They all got off the see-saw and headed for the Calla Lily flower in the corner. They climbed the steps of toadstools and took turns as they sat on the top of the Calla Lily flower. They sat down, holding their hands in the air and down the stem they went! They went through the tunnel and down one of the leaves and landed on the ground. Standing in front of them was a set of swings attached to a giant mushroom. The seats were made of clam shells, gifted to the Queen from the mermaids. They all slid into the seats, as the wind began pushing them into the air. The breeze kissed their face each time the wind pushed their swings to the sky. Fairyland was filled with the energy of joy and laughter throughout the day.

They had so much fun at fairy play land, they didn't notice the passing of time.

Annabelle, noticing how long the shadows were getting, exclaimed, "Look how late it is! The sun is going down. We better head home."

Violet and Christina, stopping in their fun, exclaimed in unison, "Oh look, the sun is already turning in for the night!" Everyone hugged and headed home, except for Violet. She turned toward the meeting place of her second date with Merin.

As soon as she arrived, she was startled by a very large, black dragon with piercing blue eyes. Sitting on the dragon was her sexy date.

"Hey Beautiful, lend me your hand," he said.

Violet walked beside the dragon and reached for his hand. Merin pulled her up onto the dragon, as if it were a horse. He sat her in front, so he could wrap his arms around her.

"Meet Magik, my noble steed," Merin said.

"Hello Magik," Violet said as she reached to pet him. "What are we doing?"

"Do you want to have some fun?" he asked.

"Of course."

Violet and Merin began flying through the clouds until they landed on one. Magik lowered his wing to the ground, making a slide. They slid down, right onto the soft fluffy clouds.

Merin showed Violet that it is possible to bounce on the purple clouds in the night sky. They looked like cotton candy and felt like really soft teddy bears. They jumped together onto the largest cloud, when they fell backward the cloud covered them like bubbles bubbling over a tub. They lay there for hours. After awhile, Merin kissed her passionately, then pulled back.

"Are you ready for what's next?" he asked.

"There's more?" she asked.

"Oh yes, much more." he said as he climbed up on Magik and pulled her up with him.

Magik flew into the night until they were surrounded by the stars. As they flew through the night sky, Merin reached his hand into the air and grabbed hold of something.

"Close your eyes and open your hands," he said.

"OK?" Violet replied, curiously, doing as she was asked.

"Now you can look," he said.

She looked down at what he had placed in her hands and gasped. She was shocked at what he just handed her. A bright white orb of light sat in her hands.

"It's a star Beautiful, just for you," he said as he pulled a silver chain out of thin air, placed the star in the middle, and clasped it around her neck.

"Oh my," Violet said as she was rendered almost speechless.

"You are a beautiful star, never forget that."

"Thank you, it's gorgeous," she replied.

"You're welcome," Merin said with a smile.

Magik flew to the clouds that were closest to the moon. He lowered his wing, so they could get off.

Merin grabbed Violet's hand and asked, "Are you ready? Follow me!"

"I'm not sure. What else could make this more perfect?"

Merin let go her hand as he walked to the edge of the cloud and stepped off. Violet screamed as he disappeared. Then saw him rising back up, a stone step beneath him. He reached for her hand and pulled her onto the stone beside him, urging her to follow and trust him, as he raised his foot to step up. With every level, the next step became visible. Violet counted a hundred steps to the top of the staircase.

"Here we are."

Violet was in complete shock and mesmerized, she felt as though she were dreaming.

"I'm in a dream, that I don't want to wake up from," she said.

"It's not a dream, it is real. You are here with me and we are really standing on the moon." He said, smiling.

Merin grabbed her around the waist with both hands and pulled her close. He took her right hand and they danced, swaying side to side, front to back. He twirled her in circles and then turned her back into his arms. He dipped her back over his arm and kissed her. Violet caressed his hair with her left hand as the kiss deepened.

Merin then gently laid her down, inside a crater, without their lips breaking contact. He caressed the side of her face and stared deeply into her eyes. He wanted to know her and her soul.

"You are so damn beautiful, I can hardly stand it. This is only our second date yet I feel like I've known you all my life. We have a connection, can you feel it?" he asked.

"Yes I can, I feel like I'm drawn to you like a moth to a flame. This has been amazing and I have no words to describe it," Violet replied.

Merin lifted Violet up to sit with him as they admired the galaxy of stars and the rainbows of the Universe. He held her tight as she rested her head back toward his chest. Violet could not believe her eyes, mind or heart. She was falling for this mysterious man, not actually comprehending that Merin had fallen for her the moment they first locked eyes.

When it was time to go, Merin led her down the stepping stone steps. Violet felt like Cinderella coming down the steps to meet her prince, except her prince was beside her with every step. The sleeves of her dress brushed against Merin's hand, the hem of her dress grazing each stone behind her as they descended down the stairs. Magik was waiting to take them back down to reality.

Back in Fairyland, Merin lifted her off his dragon and embraced her in a passionate goodnight kiss.

"So out of all your fairy tales, what is the most magical thing you would have liked to experience yourself?" he asked.

"Hmm, let me think," she said, placing her finger on her chin as they stood in silence for a few moments. "I guess Aladdin's flying magic carpet. Why?" she asked.

"Meet me tomorrow night and your wish is my command." Merin said mysteriously, as he disappeared.

Chapter 7

A Wish Granted

Violet was startled awake when a large drop of water hit her face. Wondering where that came from, she peered over the flower and saw at least twenty fairies throwing dew drops, as if they were having a snowball fight. As Violet watched in amusement, another drop hit her. Hearing laughter, she looked around to see where the dew drop came from. A piece of material blowing in the wind gave away the culprit, who was hiding behind the stem of a mushroom.

Violet decided to join the fun. Sliding off the leaf of her flower, she found another flower with a perfect dew drop, glistening in the sun. Taking the drop in her hand, she held it high in the air, pulled back her arm and let it fly towards the mushroom, where she had seen the orange material.

She cupped her hands around a drop that was sitting on a flower. Raising her hand high in the air, she pulled back her arm, and let it fly. The drop went flying in the direction of the laughing fairy, who had just thrown another drop at Violet.

"Hey Violet, I'm sorry. Did I wake you?" Christina asked, snickering.

"Yes you did, and you're not sorry!" Violet exclaimed, grinning from ear to ear.

"Nope, you're right. We are just getting started!" Christina giggled.

"OK, well lets go for it then." Violet replied.

Violet picked up a dew drop and threw it across the forest. It soared through the air, and hit another fairy in the back of the head. This fairy had on a sparkling silver dress and light brown hair. The fairy turned around to see who had hit her.

"Oh no! I'm so sorry!" Violet gasped.

"It's OK, Sweetie," the queen said.

The queen picked up a drop and launched it straight at Annabelle, who ducked down playfully behind a mushroom, attempting to avoid getting hit. The drop landed squarely on top of Annabelle's head. Annabelle picked up two drops, one for each hand. Like a pro, she aimed and hit both of her targets – Christina and Violet. Dew drops in hand, they were ready for war.

Aiming for Annabelle, Christina threw a large drop of dew, which missed the intended target and hit a gorgeous man in the face just as he stepped directly into the path of the droplet. Christina stopped in her tracks, wide-eyed.

"Oh my!" she whispered.

The man just looked at her with a grin. It was then Christina realized she was in trouble. He jumped off the tree branch and ran toward her. Christina took off running as the dark skinned man chased her through the forest. Violet and Annabelle took off chasing the Queen in the opposite direction. The forest looked as if it was raining in all directions as the dew drop fight went on.

The queen finally stopped running as she had nowhere else to run. Annabelle and Violet slid down a blade of grass as if they were sliding down a water slide. They threw their last dew drop; the queen braced herself for yet another cold shower. However, the drops simply evaporated in the bright morning sun rays.

"I'm going to find Christina," Annabelle said, as she took off skipping.

"So, have you had fun?" the queen asked.

"Oh yes, I've had a blast, thank you!" Violet gushed.

"I'm so glad. See, us fairies help humans by tending to the gardens and things like that. We also love to play and have fun. It is a very important part of being a fairy. We play like children, even as adults. It keeps our spirits bright and happy. Laughter is the best medicine, as they say, it keeps discord and depression at bay," the Queen explained.

"Yes, My Queen. I understand. I love to have fun." Violet replied, grinning.

"Oh sweetie that it so formal, call me Cassandra. Come walk with me," she said, as she turned toward the waterfall.

"You are becoming more of a free spirit and that is beautiful to see. I'm sure you wonder why you are such an introvert in your mortal life, and why you have problems in large groups?"

"Yes Cassandra," Violet agreed, "and no one understands it. They think that I'm being ridiculous!"

"Oh no honey, you're an empath."

"What's an empath?" Violet asked.

"An empath is someone who can feel the emotions of others and make those emotions their own. You can't always tell the difference between your emotions and theirs. You soak up other people's emotions like a sponge, without noticing."

"Oh wow, really?" Violet questioned.

"Yes. It is a lot to handle at times. You have a heart of gold and it is pure. Everything can easily affect you, because you have such a huge heart."

"I feel as though I do, yet I always feel so emotional and I hate feeling like a crybaby," Violet said.

"You are extremely sensitive, due to being an empath. You must remember you have a special gift."

"What gift do I have?" Violet asked.

"Well, your heart and spirit is a gift. Being an empath is a gift, also. It is not a bad thing, rather being an empath is a positive gift. You do have another gift. You will figure that one out on your journey." Cassandra said.

"I have no idea what it could be, yet I'm excited to learn more about it," Violet said.

"You should be, and it takes patience and guidance," Cassandra said.

"Guidance?" Violet asked.

"Yes dear, I would like you to meet Charming," Cassandra said, as she took a seat on a large stone by the water.

As Violet took a seat beside Queen Cassandra, who pointed to a bright green frog, sitting on a lily pad.

"I'm going to leave you alone to talk," said Cassandra, as she flew off into the distance.

"Hello, Violet," the frog croaked.

"Hello, Charming. Nice to meet you."

"We meet again," croaked the frog.

"Again?" Violet asked.

"Oh yes, of course. I could never forget someone like you."

"Awe, well thank you, when did we meet? I don't recall."

"In your back yard when you were younger, maybe like nine or ten years old. You picked me up and called me Charming. You patted my back and talked to me just like I was your friend. You held me and cried about how you wish your nightmares would go away. You really didn't have a lot of friends or family around except your grandpa. You made it clear to me how much you loved him. I croaked and tried to tell you that I will talk to someone and make it better for you. You couldn't understand me because you were already growing up and out of the magical child stage."

"Oh my goodness, Charming. I do remember you! Wow! Fairyland seems to be a place full of *my* memories."

"Those memories are returning because it's time for you to learn about who you really are." said Charming.

"And who am I?"

"Well, you're Violet." Charming croaked.

"Uh. Yeah I know that. Violet is just my name," she said, feeling disappointed.

"Yes dear, and it means so much more. Oh well I have to go. Time for lunch."

"Oh, OK, see you later?" Violet questioned.

"Yes, you will," Charming croaked, as he hopped into the pond with a splash.

As the sun started to set, she realized she needed to get ready for her next date with Merin. Violet looked into the waterfall to see her reflection and to freshen up. Then she walked toward their meeting place. When she arrived, Merin was sitting on what appeared to be a leaf from a elm tree.

"Hey Beautiful, come and have a seat in front of me," he said.

"Um, OK, why are you sitting on a leaf?" she asked as she took a seat in front of him. She nestled her body between his legs. He pulled her close and wrapped his arms around her. He leaned in and softly whispered in her ear.

"Your wish!" he exclaimed.

"My wish? What wish?" she asked, puzzled.

"A flying, magic carpet!" he answered gaily.

"But this is a leaf," she said sarcastically.

'Well, yeah, I know and this is Fairyland, so I had to improvise."

"OK. Really, it can fly?" she asked, smiling.

"Of course! With a little magic, anything is possible," he replied.

Merin kissed her neck ever so gently as if his lips were like a feather. He softly ran his fingertips down her arms and wrapped his hand tightly around hers.

"I'm never letting you go, however, you might want to hold on!" He exclaimed just as the leaf flew into the air. Fireflies surrounded them that night, as if they were lanterns. As the leaf flew higher into the night sky, the fireflies disappeared and the moon lit their way.

"Wow, your eyes are so beautiful, especially in the moonlight." Merin said.

"Thank you. Where are we going?" Violet asked.

"You will soon see."

"It's always secrets with you," she jested, smiling.

"Of course! That is part of the fun, you being surprised and not having a clue. I like it that way."

"Well I don't. OK, well sometimes I do, it just depends," she replied.

"OK. So, how have you liked my surprises so far? Let me answer for you. You love them and are amazed. I take your breath away and give you butterflies." said Merin

"Yes. How did you know?" Violet asked.

"Because I feel all of it, too." he replied.

"How is that anyway?" she asked curiously.

"Because I am magic, and the moment our lips touched we were truly connected - heart and soul. I can feel and see how beautiful of a heart you have. I can feel your soul as if it were my very own. I am an empath as well. With you, its different. I don't want to scare you away."

"I'm not scared. I feel safe. I'm nervous and shy, not scared," she replied.

They began flying in circles with the wind in her hair. They flew around for a long time, enjoying the sight of the stars and the universe. They eventually landed on the rings of Saturn. Violet turned her head toward his and they kissed. Both of their hearts began to skip a beat. Merin supported her head and looked deep into her eyes.

"You know what, Beautiful?" he asked.

"What?"

"Your kisses are so sweet and perfect, and no one could ever feature a kiss like that in the most romantic of poems. Some would spend their lives looking for an angel. They wish they would even have a chance to be close to one. I have found my angel," he said.

"I'm not an angel, or a fairy or anything like that. I'm just a mortal girl on a journey in Fairyland."

"Oh Beautiful, you are so much more than that. Now get ready!" he exclaimed.

They took off on the rings of Saturn circling around and around on the rings like a roller coaster in the sky, as Merin held her tight.

"So how is this for a wish?" he asked.

"I never asked for a wish! It is amazing!" she replied.

"Well close enough, just not a carpet," he said.

"Its pretty awesome. I love it," she said.

"I'm glad, I love to make you smile," he said.

"Me too," Violet said, smiling.

Chapter 8

Danger

Violet started off her day by running through the forest with Annabelle, Christina, and Christina's new man, Alastar. The sun was shining through the trees as they ran freely with the breeze whistling past them. Violet could hear footsteps behind her, however she didn't look back, she needed to keep her focus forward so as not to run into a tree.

The footsteps got even closer, strong arms wrapped around her waist, and gripped her tight.

"Hello, my Beautiful Paramour," he whispered in her ear. While holding her tight.

"Want to go for a ride?" asked Merin.

"Not sure, one moment," Violet said.

"Hey, do you guys care if I go for a quick ride?" Violet asked the girls.

"No, sweetie go ahead. We will see you later, have fun." the girls said urging her to go.

"Christina. Annabelle. I would like you to meet Merin." Violet said grinning from ear to ear.

"Hello, nice to meet you," Merin said.

"Nice to finally meet the man who makes her smile!" Christina laughed.

"Oh stop," Violet said, blushing.

"It's true," said Annabelle.

"Oh I know, and she makes me smile, too," said Merin.

"I can see that," Christina and Annabelle said in unison.

"Of course. I can't stop smiling," he said.

"Well, we will leave you two alone," the girls said, as they scampered off to catch up with Alatar.

Merin called for Magik to come down from flying around in the sky.

"Magik!" he called for him telepathically.

Magik came swooping down to give them a ride.

'*I will show them how I fly,*' Magik thought, grinning to himself.

Merin picked up Violet and set her on Magik's back, and then climbed up after.

'Hold on!' Magik told Merin, wickedly.

They soared through the tree tops. Magik flew so fast, they felt as though they were on a roller coaster. Magik flew up and down, up and down just like going over several hills. He quickly shifted sideways to fly between two mountains. Magik decided to show off even more, so he did a front flip. The ride took them upside down, then back around.

Not only was Violet having fun, she enjoyed how her heart soared just like the dragon soaring through the sky.

Suddenly, the clouds grew heavy and darkness loomed over Merin and Violet. Lightning strikes and loud claps of thunder filled the sky. The sky lit up electric blue – like fire, yet dark. The black clouds began enveloping Merin and Violet.

"What is going on? I'm scared!" Violet cried.

"Don't fear, Beautiful, I am here and I will keep you safe." He assured her. However, he, himself, was clueless as to what was going on.

Just as Merin gripped Violet tighter, the black clouds darkened and the wind blew harder, separating them, pulling them away from each other, twisting and turning like a tornado. Violet was thrown violently through the sky and began falling faster and faster toward the ground with nothing to break her fall. In the distance, she saw a black object flying furiously toward her. '*This is the en*d,' she thought to herself, just as Magik caught her on his back and took her to safety.

"I'm so glad to see you!" Violet exclaimed breathlessly. "I was so frightened!"

Magik took her to a bridge and told her telepathically to stay there, so he could go find Merin. Violet sat underneath the bridge shaken and afraid, crying silently. Violet was so worried about her Merin; she was praying that he would be OK.

Magik found Merin unconscious on the mountains. Magik breathed breath into Merin to bring him back to life. Merin came to and immediately asked about Violet. Magik told him that she was OK. Then explained that Zane was to blame for this storm.

"Take me to my Paramour please," begged Merin, as he slowly climbed aboard Magik's back.

Magik took Merin to where Violet sat huddled under the bridge. Merin slid off Magik and ran toward her. As soon as Merin touched Violet's hand, the darkness faded. The sun came out and all was well again in Fairyland. Violet collapsed into Merin's arms and began sobbing.

"Oh Merin, my knight in shining armor, I thought I had lost you!" she cried.

"Of course not," he said and grabbed and kissed her as if it was their last kiss. He kissed her so passionately that her knees grew weak. "I'm so glad that you are OK. I couldn't go on, knowing something happened to you, especially while with me!" he whispered.

"What *was* that?" Violet asked.

"It was my father coming after me and my happiness," Merin said in disgust.

"What do you mean?" Violet asked.

Merin took a breath, and decided to tell her the truth.

"My father is Zane, the man believed to have killed the king. Not only that, he taught me many dark ways before I turned 16. He taught me to use black magic to get whatever I wanted, as well as abducting fairies. Ever since I was little, around five years old, I would cross over and grab fairies and bring them back to the castle. They then became a servant or a soldier of his. I had no idea that anything was wrong because it was all I knew – what I had been taught. After I met you, I knew that fairies were not as he portrayed them to be. They are not dark and mischievous, rather they are full of love and light.

"But I'm not a fairy," she interrupted.

"Well, yes, you are. You are love, light and everything beautiful and perfect. You are everything I was told did not exist."

"After a couple of the fairies had told me that my father was evil and what he had done to the king, I ran away, just me and my dragon. Magik told me Zane felt betrayed because I was his only way past the edge of the Dark Forest. Somehow, he has become a stronger sorcerer and is after me."

"Oh no," Violet said.

"I know, Beautiful," he said as he stared into her eyes and caressed her face.

"So what do we do?" Violet asked.

"We do nothing, there is no way I can defeat him. I can not risk your life again. You must leave."

"But I love you!" Violet cried.

"And I love you," he said.

"Then what is the problem?" Violet demanded.

"Violet, I can never risk you getting hurt because of me!" he exclaimed.

"You called me by my name for the first time ever!" she cried.

"Because you need to listen carefully. You are a part of me and I of you. We were connected the moment our lips touched. I will always be with you, even if you can't see, or hear me. I will always be there to watch over you. I will always be with you – in your heart and in your dreams. We just can't be together in the flesh, like we are now." Merin said, as tears rolled down his face.

"Merin please, don't leave me," she pleaded. "I love you!"

"You are in grave danger with me," he said.

"Endanger me then! I don't care as long as I'm with you!" she screamed, tears rolling down her face and dripping off her chin.

"Oh, how I would love that. I can't protect you from my father, or even protect myself for that matter." Magik gently nudged his shoulder, reminding Merin its time to go. Merin slowly let go of Violet's hand and kissed her one more time. "I will always love you and remember how your kisses feel upon my lips. You are a part of my soul, so I am not completely leaving you," Merin explained.

"So what! You pull me in, I fall for you and you push me away because you are scared?" She yelled!

"Listen Violet. It is not so much that I'm scared, it is that I couldn't live my life if something were to happen to you because of me." With one last look at her he said, "Go Magik." and Magik took Merin away.

Violet ran towards the portal, tears streaming down her face, creating puddles behind her. Violet was so heartbroken, she felt as if her heart had been ripped from her chest and she couldn't breathe. She ran into the tunnel and through the door—back into the mortal world of her own garden.

Violet's knees weakened with each step. Suddenly Violet could not take another step and she collapsed onto the ground, curling up into a ball as she laid her head on the grass.

'He said he would never hurt my beautiful heart. How could he do this after everything? My life will never be the same. He swept me off my feet and let me drop, shattering me into tiny pieces.' She cried to herself, as a burst of rain came from the clouds, like the sorrow pouring from her heart.

Violet woke up in her own bed with tear stains upon her face. She could barely open her eyes. They were swollen shut from all the crying. It was then that she realized that it was not just a bad dream. The truth began to sink in and she cried herself back to sleep.

KNOCK! KNOCK! "Wake up, Violet," her mom called, through the closed door.

"What's going on mom?" Violet asked, as she opened the door to see her mom's upset face.

"It's your grandpa, he went to the hospital last night and didn't make it." she sobbed.

"Oh no! No! No!" Violet cried, running into her mother's arms.

"I know, Honey. The cancer ate away at his lungs so fast, there was nothing they could do!"

Violet hugged her mom tightly, she was in complete shock. '*Why is all of this happening now?*' she thought to herself.

"The funeral will be tomorrow at St. James Church." Mom's voice broke through her thoughts.

"Mom, is there anything I can do?"

"Yes. You could write a little something to read during the service," her mom replied, shakily.

"OK, I will get right on that," Violet said, gently nudging her mom out the door. Violet needed to be alone with her thoughts.

Violet grabbed her journal and pen and began to write a letter to her grandpa, as she recalled their memories.

Dear Grandpa,

I just want to say that I love you. I'm sad that you are no longer here, yet I'm happy that you won't have to suffer anymore.

I'm sitting here writing this to read at your funeral trying to figure out what I should write down.

I remember how I used to collect cans for you so that you could take them to the recycle center. Once a month I would bag all of them for you and you even gave me a dollar or two for helping you. I never knew how much good you did for the world, until now. You even made some awesome stuff from old wood that looked new.

Around Christmas time you would always give me a can of old fashioned candy. Some of the candy was really good and some was absolutely awful! Yet I never complained, because I loved you so and I knew you gave me the gifts because you loved me back.

You were a joker, always telling jokes and making people laugh. Like that time you called mom at three in the morning and you asked her "Did you know my friend George died?" and mom said, "Oh, no! George who?"

"George Washington," you said, and laughed hysterically.

I will miss everything, like the smell of Old Spice when I would hug you. You were always wearing that light blue hat.

 When I think about you, I think about you wearing your favorite red flannel shirt and cigarettes in the left pocket. I will miss that sweet smile on your face and those bright blue eyes. You will be missed and we love you.

Chapter 9

Spirit

The sun was going to sleep, as Violet followed the moonlight through the trees. She knocked on the door and there was no answer. She looked down and below her feet lay a key. Picking up the key, she placed it in the keyhole and turned it. Once the door opened she took off running through the forest to the waterfall. Violet sat by the waterfall listening to the croaking of frogs and the music of the crickets.

"Violet, what is wrong sweetheart?" a familiar voice croaked from the darkness.

"My heart is breaking into a million pieces. I can't breathe, I feel like my heart is being ripped from my chest. I want all of this pain to go away!" she cried.

"Sweetheart I'm so sorry, I can feel your pain. I know just what you need," Charming said.

"What is that?" she asked.

"You need a kiss from a frog," he said jokingly.

"Uh, OK?" Violet said as she picked up Charming and planted a kiss on his mouth.

"I just wanted to see if you would, plus it makes my day getting a kiss from a beautiful girl like you," he croaked.

"Oh, well you are welcome," she said feeling very confused.

"On a serious note. I really can help you. Kissing me will now give you protection on your next journey. There is a turquoise stone that can be yours, to help you heal, protect you, find your inner peace and so much more. You do have to find it on your own, though."

"How do I find it?" she asked, intrigued.

"Go to the top of the forest on the hill, there you will find a guide to help you along your way."

"Thank you Charming," Violet said and kissed him again before setting him back on his lily pad.

Violet began walking to the forest on top of the hill. She was tired by the time she got halfway there. She took a seat between two trees. The wind blew past her and Violet heard Merin's voice in the flight of the wind.

"My beautiful paramour," the wind whipped in circles around her, as if in an embrace. "My heart aches for you. Heart – something I never knew I had until you. I'm so sorry, I can't chance hurting you," the voice of the wind said.

"I love you. I don't care what you feel you need to do to keep me safe. It's my life, my choice. Please come back," Violet screamed into the wind.

"My Violet, I understand you, I want to come. You have no idea what darkness lurks around me and I won't chance that. I would rather not be with you, than to know the path I lead would forever endanger you. I will always be with you, inside your heart and spirit. Like a flame to a candle – when the fire separates from the top of the wick for brief moments, like when we are not together, yet connected at the bottom. The flame dances around and then comes in for a kiss and embrace then away again. They are always connected – like our souls. We may not be together in the flesh, yet we are always connected, even when apart from each other," he explained.

"I hate this! I just want you here with me, forget about danger. What is the use of our love when we can't be together?" She said, beginning to sob.

"I love you always. I'm here, we can see each other in dreams and talk in spirit." He said as the wind kissed her lips and then everything became still again.

"Damn you, I don't care if you are in my heart and in my dreams. I don't want you only there. I don't want to feel this pain and heartbreak. I had some amazing moments with you. You showed me a new world, a wonderful world full of magic, yet I want to erase it all!" she screamed into the wind!

Violet wiped away her tears, took a breath and continued to climb to the top and there, waiting for her, was a hawk.

"Hello my dear child, I have been waiting for you. My name is Spirit," the hawk said, as soon as she saw Violet.

"Hello, my name is Violet."

Spirit Hawk began to speak:

"Violet, beyond these trees is a journey like no other that you have ever been on before. Once you walk into this forest, I cannot help you. No one on this side can help you. I can only give you guidance here and now. Listen close to what I say.

Find your inner peace. Breathe, pay attention to everything around, yet don't let the surroundings distract you. Some things that you will hear and feel are just illusions. Remember this, *fear is just an illusion*. Repeat that with me, "Fear is just an illusion." You were full of love before you were taught how to fear and be fearful. Before you go through on your journey, there are some things you need to know.

1. There will be twists and turns, just like in life.

2. You need to seek your inner spirit and remain calm.

3. Keep your focus and don't get lost in your fears.

4. Visualize what you want to obtain and do that.

"Let's do a quick meditation to get you centered before you set out on this journey. ... Sit with your legs crossed, like a pretzel. Close your eyes and take a deep breath. Inhale, hold to the count of 4 -- 1 2 3 4," Spirit counted. "Exhale. 1 2 3 4. Continue to breathe in this manner, feel your breath and the spirit within you.

Visualize the love and light within you, Violet. What you are, no one can take that away from you. You are divine. Keep breathing and notice how your breath stops and starts, while feeling a circle of energy flowing through you; from the root chakra, at the base of your spine, to the crown chakra, at the top of your head, and back around.

Breathe in deep and open your Heart Chakra. Chakras are energy centers within your body, from the base of your spine to the top of your head. Each chakra has its own vibrational frequency. They are like spinning wheels of energy. When they are properly aligned, you can feel strong and fearless.

Now, just breathe and take in the fresh air for a few breaths and as my voice is silent, listen to the sounds around you."

Violet heard sounds of the wind, and the tree blowing, water flowing in the distance, birds chirping, it sounded so peaceful.

(15 minutes passed, with the only sound that of nature all around.)

"Now slowly open your eyes, take one more deep breath and come back to this moment, here in the meadow at the edge of the forest. How do you feel?" Spirit asked.

"I feel refreshed – like I can take on the world. I feel like a feather," Violet replied.

"Good! You will need to remember this feeling and focus on your task as well as your journey. If, you feel fear as you journey in the Dark Forest, remember, you are love. Love banishes fear. If you feel fear, hold your hand out in front of you in the STOP position, take a breath to center yourself, invoke your I AM, and banish whatever it is that is causing you to feel fear. You will know the words you need to speak. Remember, illusion abounds in the Dark Forest. Yet, there is no need to be fearful.

It's time; walk through the tree split in two," Spirit pointed toward the tree with her wing. "You have to step over and through it, then a portal will open for you. And you will be in the Dark Forest, separate from this world. No one from here can help you."

Violet turned, and without hesitation, walked toward the tree that stood before her. It looked like one tree that grew in two different directions. Violet turned for one last wave to Spirit, before stepping through the tree. She stepped her right foot through then her left. Now, with both feet on the ground, she turned to look back – and the tree was gone! She was alone in the Dark Forest! A place where no fairy was supposed to ever go.

As soon as she saw the portal was closed, fear began to set in. Violet completely forgot what Spirit had taught her, only moments before. The light began to disappear. Shadows began swirling around and creeping across the tiny rays of light that were still there. Violet heard loud howling that sounded like a pack of wolves. The sound was getting closer and closer. A large shadow within her vision caused her heart to race and her breathing quickened; she felt like she was going to have a panic attack.

Violet wanted to run and hide but couldn't. She felt paralyzed and couldn't move. The darkness held her down, like a rope was wrapped around her wrist and her body tied to a tree. She opened her mouth to scream for help – not even a whimper came out.

Here in this darkness, the fear was intense, she felt she had no voice, and no ability to move. The howling got louder and she could hear the rustle of leaves crunching beneath their paws. They were coming for her. The temperature was dropping and she could feel the coldness, like ice, surrounding her skin.

Violet closed her eyes for a split second. When she opened her eyes again, there was a pair of glowing, bright green eyes staring at her. The color of the wolf's eyes reminded her of the green forest and then it walked closer to her, snarling.

Closing her eyes, she felt a familiar energy, and then remembered Spirit's teaching. She took a few deep breaths, and holding her hand up as Spirit had instructed, said quietly, "I am love and light. May the fear be gone. You are not welcome here, I banish you!"

As soon as she said this, the snarling stopped and all was silent. She opened her eyes to see that the wolves were gone, as was her fear.

A nearby star shining brightly through the darkness illuminated a red dragon. She gasped in surprise as she saw a flash of color in the Dragon's claws. She realized the dragon held within its claws the turquoise stone she sought. It was small, round, smooth, and flat on one side.

Violet was not afraid, for there was something about him that reassured her. His blue eyes held something deep within them. As she walked closer to the red dragon, he turned over his foot and opened his claws. He held the stone out towards Violet, as if inviting her to take it.

He watched her intently as she came closer to him. He was shocked that she did not show fear. Red Dragon was glad she did not seem too fear him, because he meant her no harm. She had nothing to fear. Before she picked up the stone, she laid her hand on his head and he bowed to her. Violet bent down to place a kiss on his head. "Thank you!"

As she reached down to pick up the stone, she could feel the magic within it. It had a warm and slightly electric feeling in her hand, that flowed through her whole body.

When she looked up, the dragon that had stood before her was gone, and in its place stood a man in a crimson red cloak. He removed his hood and a shaved head was illuminated by the starlight, his eyes glowing bright blue in the light of the full moon. He stood about six feet tall and was built very strong and muscular, as she could see the muscles showing through his cloak.

"Where did the dragon go?" she asked the man.

"Your kiss has awakened me. May I ask what you need the stone that you are holding in your hand for?" he asked quietly.

Violet, forgetting about Spirit's warnings about not getting distracted and about the illusions of Dark Forest, sat there with him and told him the whole story about Merin and of her grandpa's passing.

"I wish I could just erase it all – well all of my memories and feelings for Merin, that is!" she cried passionately.

"It can be erased," he replied.

"Really, how?"

"Magic," he said.

"Oh no! I don't want to fall for that again!" she exclaimed, taking a step back.

"No love, I'm serious. It was magic that made you see and feel that way. So magic can take it all away," he said.

"OK." She said, hesitantly. "Then yes, I want the memories of Merin gone. How do I make that happen?" she asked, all hesitation gone.

"I can erase all of your memories of him, and the stone will heal your heart as you forget each memory, one at a time."

"What do you need to do?" she asked.

"Close your eyes," he said.

Violet closed her eyes waiting in anticipation. Ronan placed one hand on her face and he placed his lips on hers. Violet felt electricity start from her lips and then travel down to her feet. It was exhilarating, she felt warm and safe. She kissed him back and it intensified the power. There was no way of knowing what was happening and she didn't care. He pulled her in to a tight embrace as her knees got so weak that he had to hold her up, or she would have collapsed on the ground. He pulled away and looked into her eyes.

"I'm Ronan, and one day you will be mine."

"Oh yeah? You seem pretty confident," she said, struggling to cover up how the kiss had affected her.

"I am. We were meant to be together, its fate. We are soul mates."

"Oh? How is that?" she asked.

"Do I not make you weak in the knees, and don't you feel warm and protected? Doesn't it feel like you've known me your whole life?" he asked.

"No," she said lying.

"You can't lie to me, love. I know, I can feel, and this is no magic. It is real," he replied.

"How is it not magic? It sure felt that way," she said.

"Yes. However, do you feel anything like you did before?"

"No," she admitted.

"OK, so you know how it feels to be enchanted by magic and you don't feel that. This is different. You feel a piece of your heart is no longer missing," he stated, with arrogant confidence.

As Violet dazedly nodded 'yes' to his statement, Ronan grabbed her hand. "Walk with me."

Violet held his hand as he began to lead her to a fluorescent, blue, glowing water source.

"What are we doing?" she asked.

"We are going to help you erase memories and give you back energy that Merin has taken from you," Ronan said.

"He took energy?" she asked.

"Yes, when someone makes a connection, an invisible cord of energy is formed that connects you to the other person. This water will break the connection that you wish to let go of and forget."

"Oh wow! there is so much to a magical world!" she exclaimed, still feeling dazed.

"Yes, and the energy also applies in the mortal world, too. It is just that most mortals are not open minded enough to see and feel it. Everyone has magic within them. Energy is all around. Everything is made of energy. And magic is energy."

Ronan took off his cloak and on his back was a huge tattoo of a red dragon that looked just like him in dragon form. Violet placed her hand on his back and the dragon within his skin slithered under her touch.

"Is the dragon really moving?" she asked, astonished.

"Yes love, I am a shape-shifter," he said.

"A what?" she asked in confusion.

"I can switch from dragon to man whenever I want – mostly," he replied.

"How is that?" she asked.

"Well I was cursed to be a dragon the rest of eternity. The Queen was only able to banish half of the curse, making me a shape-shifter, which can be kind of cool."

"How were you cursed? And why?" she asked, curious to know his story

"After our father died a poisoned death when we were teenagers, my brother, Zane, cursed me and changed me into a dragon. To this day we have no idea who poisoned our father. I was the favorite son and Zane hated that, so here I am."

"The Queen found me hiding behind the waterfall. When she touched me, I was able to telepathically tell her what happened. The Queen knew there was a man beneath the dragon and although she attempted to banish the whole curse, she could not."

"I'm glad that she was able to help you with the curse."

"Me too," he replied.

Ronan walked straight into the water, as if he was walking into an ocean off the beach. Ronan submerged himself in the water and Violet began to follow.

A clear, crystal butterfly, was fluttering near her ear, gently whispered. "Don't' do it. He is Zane's brother and a master manipulator."

Violet stood frozen in her tracks, she let go his hand and pulled back away from him.

"What's wrong, love?" he asked.

"I don't want to get my dress wet," she lied.

"It's OK, it will dry," he said.

"No that's OK, I don't want to," she said.

"GET IN THE WATER!" he shouted and his eyes turned red with fire.

Violet was shocked, unsure of what to do, she held out her hands to brace herself. The next thing she knew was an arrow flew from behind her, it hit Ronan in the chest and he exploded into dust. When she turned around to see where the arrow had come from, she was stunned at who held the bow, and tears began rolling down her face. Violet collapsed in shock. Merin caught her in his arms before she could hit the ground.

Picking her up, he carried her out of the Dark Forest, back into the bright sunshine of a Fairyland meadow.

Chapter 10

A Million Pieces

Violet opened her eyes and saw Merin holding her. Tears of joy and sadness ran down her face. Violet pushed Merin away.

"How and why are you here?" she cried.

"You were in trouble," he stated, as if the logic of that should be obvious to her.

"How did you know I was in trouble?" she asked." You left me!"

"Because, we are connected and as soon as I felt your fear, I came to you. I'm sorry you had to endure my uncle causing you trouble," he said.

"Your uncle?"

"Yes, and honestly I thought he was still locked away in the dungeon in my father's castle."

"Why was he in a dungeon?" she asked.

"Well, my father told me that Ronan is the one who killed the king. The Queen thought it was my father and banished him to the Dark Forest. Ronan went after him and my father put Ronan, his brother, in the dungeon, claiming he was the one who had killed the king, which Zane said was his best friend, or so I'm told."

"What do you think?"

"Honestly? They are both horrible!" Merin exclaimed in disgust.

"I would agree with that!"

"Yes, and I believe that the Queen knows what she is talking about, she is very intelligent. Although I do believe my father did kill the king, my Uncle is no better person than my father. As I said, they are both horrible."

"I'm sorry," she said.

"Sorry for what?" he asked.

"That you had to endure that type of family."

"It's not your fault. Its OK."

"I know it isn't my fault, and I'm still sorry." Violet said as she hugged him.

Merin held her tight in his arms. Standing there, wrapped in the arms of her heart's desire, Violet could feel the warmth of his love.

"Violet, I never lied to you. Everything I ever said was from my heart," he said into her hair.

"Then how could you break my heart?" she demanded as she pushed away so she could see his face.

"That was never my intention."

"OK, but it hurt and felt like my heart was being ripped from my chest."

"I'm so sorry," he said as he stared into her eyes and caressed her face.

"Kiss me," Violet demanded.

Merin placed both hands on the side of her face, as he embraced her in a deep passionate kiss. A kiss full of love and I'm sorry. Passion and pain consumed him at this very moment. Tears started rolling down his face. He knew what he had to do, and he would hate and regret it for the rest of his life.

Merin sat down on the ground and Violet sat with him. He laid down under the moon and pulled Violet into his arms one last time. Violet lay with him in the light of the moon, within his warm grasp. Oh how she had missed him. The smell of him sent her heart soaring. Merin ran his fingers through her hair, and caressed her face until she fell asleep. Then he did something that would hurt him more than anything he had ever, or would ever again experience — he was letting her go, in the only way he knew how.

Merin waved his hand over her while she was dreaming. He replayed every memory of them together, like a clock turning back time. Just as each moment was over, he pulled them from her memory with his fingers and the precious memories became a foggy mist.

Once all memory of him was fully removed, Merin moved away into the forest, where he could watch over her until she woke up.

Violet woke up in the middle of the forest as a crystal butterfly kissed her nose.

"Good morning Sleepy Head! Did you happen to see a tall, dark-haired man around here?" Shimmer asked, even though she knew what Merin had done.

"No, I can't say that I have," Violet replied.

"My name is Shimmer, nice to officially meet you," said the crystal butterfly.

"Very nice to meet you. I'm Violet, and I'm sure you already know this," she said smiling.

Merin, watching from his hiding place, and hearing her words, felt his own heart shatter. Wreathing in pain and heartache, he turned his own heart to stone. He would always remember Violet, however, he could never hurt, or be hurt, again. As much as he loved her and wanted to feel her love, he knew he couldn't. So he did what he thought was best for Violet – he erased her memories so she would not feel the heartache of their separation. He never wanted her in pain of any sort. However, he would always be there as her protector—protecting Violet like an alpha wolf would protect his pack.

Chapter 11

Healing Witch

Come with me, I have someone for you to meet." Shimmer said.

Violet stood up and followed her into the sunset. The sky was painted with purple, pinks and gold's. It was such a breathtaking view.

"Where are we going?" Violet asked.

"To meet an Earth Witch," Shimmer replied.

"Really? They exist?"

"Oh yes, of course they do."

"I don't know why I'm surprised. By now I should be used to all of this," Violet said, laughing.

"Well, it still takes some getting used to, when everything is new for you."

"I guess you're right," Violet said.

They came to a stop in the middle of the wooded forest. In front of them stood a small stone cottage made of creek rock and stone. There was a chimney with smoke blowing out the top, from a fire burning inside. There were candles in every window, making the home glow with bright light. A Black cat with amber eyes stood by the door of the witch's home.

"Go ahead and knock on the door," Shimmer said.

Violet raised her hand to grab a hold of the brass door knocker, just as she brought the knocker down, the door opened.

"Come in Violet, I've been expecting you," the witch said.

"You have?" Violet asked, astonished.

"Of course. My name is Diane Willow, by the way. You can just call me Diane," the witch said.

The woman that stood before Violet had silver hair with streaks of black. Diane was not extremely tall, rather she was average height and weight and beautiful. The earth witch had beautiful hazel green eyes that sparkled with the light, and such a warm and loving smile.

Something looked familiar about this woman, then it hit her and she gasped. This women looked just liked her 5th grade teacher from elementary school.

"Are you ..." Violet began to ask.

"Yes Violet, I am," Diane said.

"Oh wow," Violet said, stunned.

"Yes, everyone in your life has a purpose in your journey. Some encounters are gifts, while others are lessons. We all have different paths. There is so much to everything that happens, for every birth and every death.

"What do you mean – every death?"

"Violet there is more than just the birth of a person and the death of a person. There are many births and deaths in life such as beginnings of any type of relationship, a new idea, or something completely new in your life. Deaths can be the end of anything, heartbreak, the death of a friendship, or ending of a job.

"Oh, I guess I never really thought about it that way." Violet replied.

"Well that is what I'm here for. I want to help you understand something. Let's go for a walk in the woods." Diane said.

Violet and Diane walked out the door and Shimmer took off in the other direction. They walked into the forest and surrounding them were hundreds of pine trees. The wind began to blow past them in a whistle, almost like a song being played by the trees, just as a musician would play an instrument. It was so peaceful and beautiful. They walked in silence for awhile just enjoying the beauty and peacefulness of the woods.

"Violet, I need to tell you something. It may be a little hard for you to understand, at first. However, it is why you are here." Diane said.

"Uh, OK?" Violet said, feeling a little scared at what she was about to hear.

Diane explained to Violet on the way back to the cabin all that had happened with Merin. She explained that Violet didn't remember, because he took those memories to protect her. Diane also told Violet that she was going to give the memories back, however, she wouldn't feel the intensity of the heartache, because her heart would stay healed, to a certain degree.

"But why would anyone want to take away such wonderful memories?" Violet asked.

"For two reasons, honestly. He loves and cares for you so much that he didn't want you to ever hurt, so he figured you would be better off not remembering. Also you wanted them, demanded them, to be erased because the pain was unbearable to you." Diane explained.

"Oh," Violet said, in complete shock.

"Yes it is a lot to take in. I believe that one should never have memories erased. Everything you go through, both good and bad, make you who you are. So when we get back I will return your memories, however, your heart will be healed from the heartache, just as it would have healed overtime. I'll just be healing it at massive speed.

"OOOO! You can do that?" Violet asked, still in shock.

"Of course I can dear," Diane said, smiling.

They arrived back at the cottage and sat down at a beautiful handmade table, made from pine wood. She could smell the scent of pine throughout the cottage.

"Violet, where is the stone that you got from the dragon?"

"It's right here," she said. Pulling the stone out of a velvet pouch, she handed it over to Diane.

Diane walked over to one of her cupboards, pulled out a little treasure box, and sat back down next to Violet. She opened the box and pulled out a silver bracelet with a charm in the shape of a frog. In the middle of the frog was an empty space perfect for Violet's little stone.

Diane took Violet's stone and placed it in the middle of the bracelet. A light appeared, and it looked as if the stone and the bracelet charm were melding together.

"Do you know what this stone does?" Diane asked.

"I know it helps with healing and protection, that is about all I know." Violet replied.

"There are many properties in this bracelet. The frog, as one of your spirit animals, also has magical properties. Some of the frogs properties are rebirth, healing, dreaming. Also some of the properties of the turquoise stone are protection, strength, love, and positive thinking.

"That's a lot of stuff!"

"Yes it is. It's very powerful," Diane said as she placed the bracelet on Violet's right wrist and adjusted it to fit by closing the clasp a little tighter.

"Thank you so much," Violet said with tears in her eyes.

"You are very welcome, my dear. Now there is one more thing before you go." Diane said as she stood up to pour a cup of tea from her cauldron hanging above the fire. Diane handed it to Violet and told her to drink it and she would remember everything when she woke up tomorrow. "Do not get up too fast tomorrow morning or you will get dizzy and may pass out from the memories flooding back." Diane advised.

"Yes ma'am," Violet said as she sipped the sweet tea of honey, ginseng and some other magical ingredients she didn't know.

They chatted a little more as Violet drank her tea. When Violet finished her tea, Diane gave Violet a loving embrace, and sent her on her way. "Take care Violet," Diane called after her.

"You do the same, thank you." Violet said with a smile and a wave, as she disappeared into the woods.

Chapter 12

Do Not Weep

Violet woke up and looking around, realized she was lying in her own bed in the mortal world. She stood up really fast and plopped back down. Memories of Merin came flooding back all at once, knocked her on her butt and left her feeling very weak and disoriented! She sat on the bed wondering what happened. Then she remembered Diane, the tea and the warning Diane had given her.

'Oh my!' Violet thought to herself. She lay there on the bed and cried for awhile.

She could now feel all the memories that had been erased. She could also feel how wonderful they were, even though she did not feel the full effect of the emotional heartbreak, as she had done before, she could still feel heartache — as if the pain had been diluted.

Knock! Knock! .... Violet was startled out of her reverie.

"Violet, are you getting ready for the funeral," her mom called through the door.

'Oh man, that's today,' she thought to herself.

"Yes, Mom. Give me ten minutes."

She had to get up and get dressed.

Violet quickly put on a gray knee length dress with a butterfly necklace that dropped down over her heart. Violet fixed her hair in curls. She had on simple silver and white eye shadow with waterproof mascara and eyeliner.

The funeral home smelled of flowers and Violet felt so much sadness. At the front of the funeral home room, her grandpa lay in a casket of dark colored wood. A USA flag was draped over the bottom half of it. On the left side, stood an easel with a poster board on it and pasted to the board were pictures full of memories. There were pictures of Violet and her grandpa and her cousin, all holding birthday cakes. Violets cake was in the shape of a 3D doll cake with a fluffy blue ball gown. The doll had long brown hair and tan skin. Grandpa's cake had blue and red flowers set on white icing. He was wearing a navy blue hat with a USA logo on it. He was wearing a red flannel shirt and the scent of old spice filled the room. His bright blue eyes and happy smile lit up the photograph.

'*I feel like he is in this room, I can smell him as if he is still here.*' She thought to herself.

Violet looked over in the corner and there stood a ghostly angelic image of Grandpa Andrew! Surrounding him was an aura of white and gold light.

"Do not weep for me, Little Bit, for I am fine. Although I don't know why people say, rest in peace. There is no such thing (he said with a laugh) The people who die, never truly die. We live on in a different dimension. However, we walk with our loved ones until we are called to another life. I will always be in your heart and I love you. I am better here than I was in the mortal world." Grandpa's ghost explained to her.

"Grandpa I wish that you were here so I could tell you all about this journey I am on and all I have been through," she whispered.

"Oh Little Bit. I know all about it, we can see all. I will be guiding you, and helping you along the way," he said, and then disappeared.

Violet stood there staring into space as she watched her grandpa disappear into a mist. Then her consciousness was in the back of the room, watching herself go through the motions of the funeral.

Her family and friends surrounded her and covered her with hugs as they said "I'm sorry for your loss."

Her eyes began to burn as she watched everyone who loved her and her grandpa show so much love and support. She hugged her family back. "Thank you, I know he is not here in the flesh, yet he is here in spirit," she said again and again.

Violet watched herself get up in front of everyone and read the eulogy for her grandpa. Tears welled in her eyes, not because of sadness this time, rather because she knew he was fine and that he would be with her always. The funeral ended and everyone got in their cars to head to the cemetery for the burial.

The car carrying immediate family pulled up behind the Hurst at the cemetery. The pallbearers carried the casket to the spot where there was a hole dug six feet deep. Each family member took a flower from the bouquet that was on his casket, as a keepsake to remember him.

Violet's Uncle was then handed grandpa Andrews' flag, since he was the oldest son. Everyone walked up to hug him as tears fell from his eyes. Violets mother picked up a wreath that was set on the right side of the funeral home. The wreath was white with little USA flags glued all the way around it. Each flag had family member's names written on it.

Violet and her mom went home, shortly after saying their goodbyes to the rest of the family. Violet went to her room and went to sleep soon after getting home. It had been a really long day, with everything that had taken place in both Fairyland and the mortal world.

Chapter 13

Fairyland Ball

Violet woke up to the loud sound of cheers that filled the air. Sitting up to find out what the noise was all about, she saw every creature in Fairyland was cheering and dancing with joy.

Christina jumped up on the flower next to her and said, "Here," handing a rolled scroll to Violet. Opening it, Violet saw, to her astonishment, that it was an announcement and invitation from Queen Cassandra.

Violet couldn't believe what she was reading. She started to ask Christina, "How . . .?"

Christina shrugged her shoulders, "A miracle." Then scampered off to deliver more invitations.

It MUST be real. It was signed by the Queen and had the Royal Seal at the bottom.

HEAR YE!
HEAR YE!

IN CELEBRATION
OF THE KING'S
RETURN

ALL LOYAL CREATURES
OF FAIRYLAND

ARE HEREBY INVITED
TO A MASQUERADE BALL

TONIGHT!

**WHEN THE MOON RISES
YOUR COMPANY IS REQUESTED
IN THE ROYAL GARDENS**

Queen Casssandra

As the sun light began to fade and the moon began to rise. Queen Cassandra appeared wearing a sparkling silver dress. The dress flowed freely and a sheer layer kissed the ground as she walked. Her brown hair was in curls and loosely pinned up.

"Violet are you ready?" she asked.

"No ma'am. I don't have anything to wear, except just what I have on." She pointed to her gray dress she had worn to grandpa's funeral.

"Oh yes dear, you most certainly require a different dress. Tonight view me as your Fairy Godmother, however, there is no clock to strike midnight. You will not have a carriage turn into a pumpkin and lose a shoe." Cassandra chuckled.

"Yes ma'am" Violet said with a chuckle

Queen Cassandra took out her magic wand and pointed it toward Violet, "Turn slowly to your right." As Violet turned, Stars swirled around her in a vortex and then everything went still as she stopped her turn, once again facing Cassandra.

Violet looked down and saw that she was wearing a turquoise satin dress with scroll-like crystal beading under her bust. The dress billowed and flowed around her legs, and the

131

straps draped lightly over her shoulders – they matched the sequined design under her bust.

On her feet were silver shoes, also covered in crystal beads. On Violet's head was headband covered in beads and pearls on her right side, her hair fixed with loose curls. Violet felt just like Cinderella at this very moment. The queen handed her a turquoise mask with sparkling glitter around the corners of the eyes.

Cassandra said, "I have someone for you to meet." As she turned and walked to the edge of the forest, where she motioned for someone to join her.

As Violet came up beside the Queen, a majestic unicorn stepped from behind her.

"You are on your way. This is Orion. He will take you where you need to go," Cassandra said as she led the unicorn over for Violet to climb upon.

"A unicorn? That's awesome! I can ride him?"

"Yes! You go ahead and get on and I will meet you at the Castle," Cassandra said, holding her cupped hands to give Violet a boost up onto Orion.

Violet climbed upon the white as snow unicorn. "Hello," she said to Orion, as she patted his head.

"Hello Violet, you look beautiful," Orion said.

"Thank you."

"Here we go, off to the ball."

Orion walked gracefully through the forest. The forest looked so beautiful and magical with the moonlight shining through the branches of the trees. They passed the waterfall, and Mermaid Lagoon, then continued on through the forest until all of a sudden Orion stopped.

When he stopped, Violet's eyes fixated on the gates made of gold with flowers that wrapped around the bars. Violet had never seen anything more beautiful. The gates opened automagically. Beyond the gates was a pathway made of moonstone. The moonlight was shining on the path in such a way that it made the moonstones glow like stars in the sky. At the end of the pathway was a gorgeous castle made of trees, river stones and crystals.

They made their way down the path to the front door, just as Violet was about to get down and knock, the doors opened. Once the doors opened, Orion walked her into the building and through the corridor that contained a grand stairway, with spiral steps that were made of stone and covered with moss-like grass.

The inside of the castle looked like the outside was living inside, there were hints of stone here, with cathedral-like columns that had vines growing around them. There were also beds of various flowers and patches of grass that had been allowed to grow wild. It was natural and fit for Fairyland; it was perfect in her eyes. Orion took Violet to the back door and out into the royal garden.

Outside, in the Royal Garden, was a huge water fountain, about the size of a house. In the fountain were mermaids and fish, swimming among the light of fireflies and fallen stars. The trees were covered in little stars of light — it was truly magical, even more magical than everything else she had seen since arriving in Fairyland.

Now she really did feel like she was dreaming. The trees looked as though they were showered in jewels that gleamed in the moonlight. Fairies, dragons and all the creatures in Fairyland were dancing to the lovely music sang by the mermaids and nature's instruments played by others.

Orion stopped next to steps so that Violet could easily dismount. Wide eyed with wonder, Violet dismounted and put her hand on Orion's flank to balance herself as she walked down the steps. He waited until she was safely down the stairs.

"Thank you for the ride!"

"You are welcome," Orion said, as he went to join his friends on the other side of the garden.

"May I have this dance?" She turned around to see a man with a mask of blue. The man was tall, with blue eyes that glowed like the mask covering the top part of his face.

Violet just stood there and stared for a moment at those eyes. They reminded her of someone's eyes that was very dear to her. Someone that she could not remember at this exact moment.

They began to dance and he twirled her around, "You look very fairy-like Violet, very fitting." he said.

"How do you know my name?" she asked. You would think by now she would figure everyone knew her name, and yet she still asked, because she was still surprised.

"Well Violet, I know because I am your grandpa," he said, reaching up to remove his mask.

Violet stopped in the middle of a turn and just stood there in complete shock and disbelief. She couldn't move. "But I went to your funeral and you were laying in a casket!"

"Yes, true. That was the mortal body. However, as I told you, no one truly dies, that is why I am here in Fairyland. This is my home. I was in the mortal world for awhile because I was killed here in Fairyland." he explained.

"But why were you killed and how could you come back?" she asked.

"Well I was killed by someone I thought was my friend. Apparently he was jealous of me and all that I had as King." He told her the story of Zane. "I'm here in Fairyland because, after you found my home, your home, I knew I could finally come back." he explained.

"How?" she was stunned.

"Well, I lost the way here and could not come back due to the poison. However, you, my dear, found the doorway!"

"The moon helped me."

"Yes. The moon is a part of you."

"Huh?" she said, feeling really confused.

"You will see," he said, mysteriously.

Queen Cassandra stood in front of the fountain "It is time, my love." she told King Andrew, holding her hand out to him.

"Yes, I suppose it is," he said to his Queen and gave Violet a smile and walked away.

"First and foremost I would like to announce that I'm glad to be back home here in Fairyland," he announced "The Queen and I have some very important news and we would like to ask Violet to come forward, please." Holding his hand out to Violet and motioning her forward.

Violet stood and had to hear her name called again before believing what she was hearing. She walked up to meet the Queen and her Grandpa who was King of Fairyland!

"Violet, you have learned so much here in Fairyland. I've had the privilege of watching you grow over the years and you have grown into a beautiful young woman. You have come into your own. You have faced heartache, and fear and you have come out stronger. You have faced the storm and didn't let it keep you down. You have learned to dance in the rain and not take anything for granted. You have learned to love and to believe. Violet, first and foremost, you are my granddaughter. You are also a fairy and today you have earned your wings and you are ready to fly!" he said, waving his hand toward her.

Violet was speechless and didn't know what to say. Wings started to sprout from her shoulder blades; it felt like feathers running up her skin. Violet turned her head to the right and the left attempting to look over her should to see what was happening.

The crowd applauded as the amethyst colored wings changed colors to match her evening dress. Tears clouded her eyes as she realized that she was a true fairy and this is why she felt so different in the mortal world, because she was a fairy and didn't really belong there. She was one of the magical creatures you read about as a child. A creature that children pretended to be. Violet was now glowing brighter than ever.

The music began to play again, and Grandpa wrapped her in a warm embrace, as Queen Cassandra joined in a family hug.

"Here you go, my sweet Violet," Grandpa proudly said with a smile upon his face, as he pulled something from out of his shirt pocket and motioned for her to turn around.

As Violet turned her back to him and lifted her hair, Grandpa-Turned-Fairy-King, placed a silver chain around her neck. Looking down, Violet saw that he had gifted her a key, to which an amethyst crystal was attached. The crystal shimmered in the moonlight.

"Thank you, it is beautiful," she said gratefully.

"You're welcome. I'm sure you are wondering why a key?" Grandpa asked, grinning widely.

"I was." Violet replied.

"You will find out soon enough," Grandpa grinned.

Violet walked toward the fountain feeling very magical. She twirled herself around in circles, watching her dress move with each spin. Her grandpa joined her for a celebration dance. They danced with the music and then the song faded and it was over. Violet gave her Grandpa a huge and loving hug. Grandpa wrapped his arms around her and spun her around, then placed her back on the ground.

"May I cut in?" asked a young gentleman, knowing that this was his chance to dance with the beautiful fairy.

"Yes, you may," said King Andrew, as he handed his granddaughter off to the tall young man. The man had dark hair, and brown mesmerizing eyes that she could see through the white, half mask he wore.

"Hello, I'm Josidian, and I would love to dance with you, if you are willing." he said, as he bowed, holding out is hand to her.

"Why yes, I would love to dance with you," she said, extending her hand. Josidian led her around the dance floor twirling her round and round.

As they danced in the garden that night, their wings began to flutter and they began to float, while wrapped together during a slow dance. She felt passion and energy between them as they rose higher and higher and before she knew it, they were dancing among the stars. Her wings were fluttering in sync with his. They danced among the stars for what seemed like hours. Everything felt so right.

Chapter 14

Moon Fairy

Violet woke up the next morning in her bed in the mortal world.

'Was it all a dream?' she questioned upon awakening. Then she felt a weight around her neck. She got up and looked into the mirror. A key with an amethyst stone dangled from the silver chain around her neck. Beside her bed was a note addressed to her.

Dear Violet,

You are probably wondering if you had a dream about being in Fairyland and / or that it was just your imagination and I'm writing to tell you that it was all real. You are a fairy. The necklace that you are wearing is a key to Fairyland and you can come home whenever you want to.

You, my dear, are a Moon Fairy, which is why the moon is a part of you. You speak to the moon; the moon calms you, and helps you. You also help the moon shine so brightly through the night with your love, light and spirit.

Love, Grandpa

Epilogue

Violet sat in the last class of her Junior year in High School. They were watching a video featuring a boring monotone announcer and Violet fell asleep, daydreaming about Fairyland. She was awakened by the lights, as the credits rolled by.

"Hey," said a familiar voice. Violet looked around to see Joe stretching sleepily. He had also fallen asleep while watching the video.

"I've been really tired lately," he explained, covering his mouth to hide a huge yawn.

"I know exactly what you mean. I've felt the same way." Violet replied, hiding her own yawn.

"Like last night – I had the strangest, yet coolest, dream that I didn't want to wake up from, because it felt so real. It felt like it was not a dream, rather that I was awake in some other world. For some reason, this video reminded me of it."

"Really, what was it about?" Violet asked her friend, Joe.

"Well, I was in this really cool castle with royalty, and this girl and I were dancing among the stars, we were flying in the sky. It was awesome!" he explained.

"That was not a dream, Josidian. That was real and the girl was me," she smiled.

About the Author:

The inspiration for this novel was to escape her own reality and within this book, Lynn created her own world. While journeying to fairyland, Lynn wrote about experiences within her own life, from a teen's point of view, growing up with a kind and sensitive heart. *Love, Light and Violet* is Lynn's story, with mystical and magical twists.

Lynn has also published a children's book *Happy Magical Dreams,* under the pen name, *Lynn Brown.*

This book was written to help her son have Happy Magical Dreams instead of the nightmares that were keeping him up at night. Lynn had many poems published in the books by poetry.com. She is currently preparing a book of her poetry to be published in the near future, with a new publisher.

Lynn began writing as way to escape her own reality. She was captivated with poetry at a young age. Lynn absolutely loves how words can be used in such a way as to invoke intense emotions and memories. Putting her emotions in words on paper, was a way to express what she was feeling.

Lynn is a Reiki Practitioner, Oneness Blessing Practitioner and a spiritual soul. She's always spreading love, light and kindness wherever she goes.

When Lynn is not working her day job, she is either spending time with her family, using her photography skills to capture magical memories or sitting in the magic of nature, expressing herself on paper.

Lynn resides in Kentucky with her husband and children. She currently works in the medical field, where she is the bright smile and kind voice that brightens the days of those in pain.

Join Lynn on a magical journey to Fairyland, you never know what awaits you!

More books are in the works for this busy and creative author.

Follow Lynn Renz:

On the web:
https://lynnbrownauthor.wixsite.com/website

Facebook:
https://www.facebook.com/lynnrenzauthor/

Instagram:
lynn renz author